ROCK
THE
PEDESTAL

SAVING MEN, WOMEN AND CHILDREN FROM PREDATORS

Joseph Harris

Destiny House Publishing, LLC

ISBN:1936867184
ISBN-13:978-1936867189

This book is designed to help people accept Jesus Christ as Lord and Savior (Romans 10:9). It is written also to remind everyone that Jesus is on His throne in Heaven and He will never be moved. Continue exalting Him, forever and ever! It is also to encourage people to come down from any pedestal of pride, high places, high mindedness, and self-centered attitudes. God wants us to be humble and caring people (1 Thessalonians 5:14). Help someone today and make a difference! It is also for you to rebuke the devil who puts himself on a pedestal. Start by asking Jesus to come into your heart today, repent of your sin and allow the transformation process to begin inside of you. Nothing is hidden from the Lord. So you can surrender to Him. He already knows you and is expecting you to ask and believe in whatever your need. We need the Holy Spirit to help us when we receive Jesus in our heart. We should desire to walk in His transforming power over spiritual battles of the heart, mind, soul and spirit. All power is in Jesus Christ who blesses us, daily. There is nothing too hard for Him!

The second part of this book (page 125) contains a story. In this story, Alex has recently left the military and joined a prosperous company to find himself in a situation leading up to a battle against evil, corruption and manipulation within his job, city and government. While working, he discovered some bad guys who kidnapped multiple women as hostages. These young women were sold into sex trafficking and prostitution. As he learns of this horrible criminal act, he is reminded in his flashback that something similar happened to his sister involving sex traffickers and prostitution. So because of this evil committed by corrupted minded men and some women behind the scene, Alex will fight as hero and one giving hope to the captive and the city. His sister was never found during a similar crisis. So when asked to help on this case, he did not hesitate.

CONTENTS

PRAY FOR A LIFE CHANGING TRANSFORMATION

Father, thank you for transforming me into a man who has a relationship with you. This transformation helps me to be free in this world and the one to come. I walk in the newness of life. I am transformed because of your mercies made new each day. I pray to walk like I am transformed and be a witness for my Lord, Jesus Christ.

Father, this book is written to give you all the glory! You are my Lord and my Redeemer. I pray that you minister to my heart and to those that read this book. Lord, I pray to worship you forever. Keep my heart in the palm of your hands. Father, keep my mind stayed on you. Give me the peace that surpasses all understanding and joy only you can give. Lord, I pray to hide your word in my heart that I may not sin against you. Lord, I pray that your word will go out and not return void and that people will be saved by giving their heart to you, today. I pray that this project will be a blessing to millions around the world. Lord, all glory praise and thanksgiving to you. In Jesus name, Amen.

PURPOSE: This book is for those who need to know the power of God in their lives. The first step is accepting Jesus as Lord (Romans 9:10). Go ahead and say to God: "Lord Jesus, I repent of my sin, please forgive me. I open my heart to you, right now. Lord, come into my heart. I receive you as Lord of my life. I believe you died for my sins and you were raised from the dead on the third day. Thank you! Hallelujah!"

It is then that the transformation process begins. God is looking for people to be transformed by His power. He is looking for us to have a closer relationship with Him. It is the transformation process that will benefit you and your family. This will please God. Transformation is a part of the process and God's will for your life. We belong to Him. He moves perfectly in our lives for His glory. Allow the word of God to change your heart. It has the power to take hold of all of your spirit, soul and being. This book is for everyone to see God as the head of their lives and depend on His awesome power and be delivered into His Kingdom. God helps us in all kinds of life situations and controversies. The intent is not only that we would witness for Jesus, but that we would be renewed in Christ and walk the faith life each day. He alone can perform miracles in our lives.

Jesus transforms people with the power of his touch and saves lives. This book shares His power of love as a priority in the lives of his people. This book will challenge you to surrender and be transformed. Allow the Lord God to take you places that you have never been. He will cause you to be on fire as a witness. He will also restore you and renew your mind.

This book is for you to pass on to your future generations so they can also be transformed and walk in the newness of life. Let them know that you care about people and want to make a difference in somebody's life today! You will be encouraged in every scripture to live a better life by walking in the spirit and having insight in the spirit realm. Every man, woman and child will learn that they can find God in their adventures. He does a good work transforming our lives. This book is designed to allow the blessings to flow in our lives it is in Jesus Christ, the risen Lord who is the head of the Church of Jesus Christ, the One who died and rose from the dead.

Repent today and ask Jesus to come into your heart and be your Lord and Savior. Trust Him forever and receive eternal life with Jesus Christ, the Son of the living God. Praise, glory, thanksgiving, and worship to His holy name.

JOSEPH HARRIS

CHAPTER 1
ROCK THE PEDESTAL

Ephesians 2:8 For by grace you have been saved through faith, and that not of yourselves, it is the gift of God.

The devil was defeated by Jesus who came with truth and grace. The devil was knocked off his pedestal because of his pride (Rev 12:7-13). He also thought it was permissible for him to steal, kill and destroy God's children (John 14). The devil was kicked out of heaven because of pride. He wanted to be God. When people are filled with pride, they are knocked off of their pedestal, as well. You should be filled with joy that God took the devil from high places to a low place called, Hell. God can rock the pedestal in the life of anyone who puts themselves higher than the next person. When God rocks the pedestal, he makes an impact. The impact is that someone will be brought low. A pedestal is a symbol of a high place. The problem with it is that people tend to treat others in a condescending and evil manner. In other words, they make others feel degraded, insignificant or less important than themselves.

Some people in high positions will rob you, rob God, strip you of your dignity, and try to influence you to deny God. Some will take from you, and in some cases, leave you for dead. Joseph's brothers left him for dead. But Joseph, because of his relationship with God, was able to impact the heart of Pharaoh. In other words, when God shows up in you, something happens. Joseph impacted the life of Pharaoh and Potiphar. Joseph received favor when God rocked the life of Pharaoh and the entire empire of Egypt. When God rocks the pedestal, your position will change in life. God advanced Joseph from the pit to the palace as second in command of Egypt. A dream will advance or propel you. God is able to rock the pedestal of every demon spirit, witch, and evil spirit that gets in the way. A dream that comes true will make others believe that God can do what He promises and speak through His word. A God-given dream will wake up your family and make them witness the power of God. God knows who he wants to put up and who he wants to bring low. Another example of the power of God is when God used David. As a young boy he was able to slay a giant who put himself on a pedestal and shouted to King Saul's army with a bully and taunting attitude; striking fear in their hearts. But God knows how to deal with people who put themselves on a pedestal. In short, David went out bold and struck him with one stone and brought him down, then took off his head. My God will fight my battles and triumph over all enemies (1 Samuel 17:50)!

Jesus makes sure that every believer knows that the only way you are saved is through faith in Jesus Christ who is full of grace and truth. Make sure you never put yourself up high on a pedestal. God rocked the devil's pedestal and He will rock your pedestal if you place yourself up high. Keep your heart on God. Stay humble and obedient in the eyes of the Lord.

Saul was knocked off his pedestal. God can humble anyone. Saul was a murderer and he put himself on a pedestal to kill every Christian he could get his hands on. God knocked him off his high horse, and then he was filled with the Holy Ghost to witness around the world in Jesus' name (Acts 2:1-4). Jesus made him a chosen vessel for God's Kingdom (Acts 9:1-16).

The favor that God pours out exceeds human favor. However, God can be in it! God can make your enemies bless you! Be a man who walks in favor! Believe it today! Grace is unmerited favor that can never be earned. God is the only giver of grace through Jesus Christ, who came to wash our sins away. Grace is given by God and distributed to all people. Do not worry; you also have favor. No one can escape grace because Jesus came by grace and truth. Grace is a blessing in our lives. It is continually given by God on a daily basis. Grace is power that gives favor from God. No one has ever earned grace through works or any other way. Grace is favor given only by God. Man does not have the power to give you grace. God provides grace every single day and never misses a moment. It's free because Jesus died for our sin. We never had a right to receive this blessed gift of grace from our Lord. Because of our sin against God, we deserve only one thing, death. However, His love extends beyond our imagination. He washed us as white as snow in the power of His love. His grace works on us even in our transformation process (Eph 2:8).

RECEIVE A SEED FROM GOD'S WORD

LUKE 8:10-12 And He said, to you, it has been given to know the mysteries of the kingdom of God, but to the rest it is given in parables, that seeing they may not see, And hearing they may not understand. Now the parable is this: The seed is the word of God. Those by the wayside are the ones who hear; then the devil comes and take away the word out of their hearts, lest they should believe and be saved.

God wants you to be a transformed man who stands tall. He will stand on your side. Be a man that sows seed in the kingdom. When you become a seed sower, you might as well get ready for the enemy to put forth his best tactics to try to steal the word from your heart. He will attempt to snatch your joy and peace. Fight back like you are in a boxing arena. Knock Him out! Once the enemy thinks that he took it from your heart then he wants your mind and your confession to be destroyed as well. The enemy will try to hinder, block, steal and conceal your blessings from God, every time. This foe is not so much concerned about taking your blessings. You are the target. You are like the fertile ground that receives new seed. The enemy does not want the word (seed) in your heart. If you get the word, then you have the power to call on Jesus. When you get the word inside your heart, which is the seed, the enemy will come up against you demanding that you step away from the ministry and your purpose. The enemy starts immediately attacking you when you accept Jesus as Lord.

I never understood those that think everything is okay when the enemy comes their way. I am so excited about the power of God's word. I remember working on a farm doing intense work. I had to deal with all the farm animals. On the farm, I learned how to be disciplined in working in so many areas. My father was responsible for placing me and my brothers on the farm to work.

One of the most important things I learned on that farm, working under the heat, was plowing the ground at the right time to put seed in it. When you plow the ground, you will always need a strong mule, dependable plow, and or a good tractor. During those years, tools were available, but Mr. Brown was old school and depended on a mule he talked to day and night. Sometimes as a youngster, I would watch him and be amazed at how that mule responded to him even after a long day of plowing. I watched Mr. Brown talk to that mule in the backyard, many times. The point is Mr. Brown was a man who knew the power of planting seed and the cost associated with planting seed.

Although, he left us to be with the Father in heaven, he was a remarkable example on how to plow to plant seed, ensuring the best outcome. Because he was wealthy in his knowledge and ability to plow and plant seed, others would be wealthy as well, especially the farm owner. I believe that we need some new ground to plow and plant. We need hearts that will receive the power of God's word penetrating on the inside and manifesting inside- out.

That farm has a special meaning in my life because it always left the power of the seed in my mind. I recall eating so many watermelons with my brothers and cousins on that farm. The one thing we tried to avoid was swallowing seeds. We use to spit them out. I always thought that if I swallowed it something would start growing inside of me. So I was extra careful. No matter how careful I was, I still swallowed some, but nothing happened.

However, when I dropped some on the ground and came back a few days later, I would some new growth. God was showing me, as a little boy, the power of what a seed can do even by just dropping it on the ground. I also learned that multiple seeds in one watermelon come from an original seed that was planted. God's word is the seed and it is the only word that can plant and produce in your life. God has a way of multiplying seed from the original seed.

Believers have to be cautious of what can happen if you allow the enemy an inch. Watch out for those who have fallen to the wayside. And watch for yourself. The enemy attacks those who claim to be saved. He comes to strip us of our freedom in Jesus Christ.

MAKE A CHOICE, GOD OR EVIL

GEN 3:5 For God knows that in the day you eat of it, your eyes will be opened, and you will be like God knowing good and evil.

You should automatically choose God! The devil should have no place in your thought life, married life, nor any area of your life. In fact, God knocked the devil off of his pedestal because of his pride, disobedience, and his rebellious and disrespectful spirit. The enemy has his own self-constructed throne. God knocked the devil and his demons off their throne and sent them to hell! So stop entertaining the enemy! The power of choice existed in Genesis Chapter 2 and Chapter 3:6-7 when Adam and Eve had to make a decision. It was to be either in obedience to God or disobedience under the persuasion of Satan and flesh (1 John 2:16). Truth be told, some people will ignore God. But the Christian knows better and must help the unbeliever choose God. Too many people choose the devil because everything feels good. Think about what feels good in your life. The choices you make count! When you get married, you either chose the right bride or she chooses the right husband. The bottom line is that you live with your choice either happy and blessed or miserable like hell.

The choices you make yield results. We bear fruit based on our choices. When we choose God, we accept Him to take hold of our lives, transforming minds, hearts and spirits. There is power in making Christ choices. Change is based upon our selection. You either have the mind of Jesus Christ or the mind of the enemy. It's a choice. Don't accept anything less than what God offers. When we are transformed to serve God, our mind comes from God only. We get this transformation because we chose God over evil. We are transformed by the renewing of our minds (according to Romans 12: 1-4). Therefore we are more prone to making better decisions in life. Your choice has a major impact on your identity and your success in life. The decisions we make can generate great results in each person's life.

The decisions we make have consequences behind them. It

was sin in the Garden of Eden that caused our eyes to be wide open. It was a choice that Adam and Eve made by listening to the enemy to eat of the fruit. God had instructed them to not eat it, but they did it anyway. This is when disobedience and rebellion entered man. The devil had already displayed rebellion, disobedience and pride in heaven against God.

Eve could not see beyond the manipulation, seduction, and deceit of the enemy at that very moment. Be careful when the enemy comes to you to seduce you into making a bad choice. Keep in mind one bad choice (as it happened in the Garden) can lead to death and sin in this life. The enemy is well known for his ability to seduce people. Seduction doesn't always take on a sexual appearance. It is being influenced through the lust of the eyes, flesh and pride resulting in one acting on what tempted them in the first place!

Before they ate of the fruit, they lived in paradise. Eve's husband, Adam had the power to deal with that old serpent on the spot. Because of one disobedient act all of our eyes are wide open. Not only are our eyes open, our lives opened up to sin. We were transformed from perfection to a sin nature. Our eyes are not opened to be like God, as the enemy tried to manipulate. Our eyes were open to sin, just as Adam and Eve recognized that they were naked. Before that one single act of sin against God, they were perfect. Instead their eyes became opened to a sin nature. Man will never hold the sight of what God can see because He is the source. Man is not God and will never be God. Man is the substance of what God made to live in harmony with what God designed for him. One mistake that the enemy did make is that the Lord God through His Holy Spirit did create us to have our eyes wide open in the spiritual realm for His purpose. The only way to access that ability is to know Jesus for yourself. So now with God, our eyes are open to see the invisible and visible. We could never see it, except for the power of God.

You will be able to see angels descending from heaven similar to Jacob's experience. He had a dream in which he saw angels back and forth on a stairway to heaven and earth, most commonly known as Jacob's ladder (Genesis 28:12). In Genesis 3:7 we read, Then the eyes of both of them were opened, and they knew that they were Naked; and they sewed fig leaves together and made themselves coverings.

Our eyes do not have to be wide open to sin. They can be open to recognize the tricks and maneuvers of the enemy. Our eyes can be used to the advantage in giving God glory.. Our eyes are to be watchful for His Holy and glorious return to earth. Now our eyes can be wide open to recognize what God wants for our lives and for His purpose. I like the words the Apostle Paul stated "We walk by faith not by sight." Even with our eyes wide open, we still need to walk by faith. Your eyes might see something, but do you really have faith for it to be manifested in the spirit. Your eyes have the power to see what God has for you and your family for the edifying of the ministry.

One of the most important things in life, along with your vision is the ability to listen. Everyone must learn to listen to God's voice only. The enemy is filled with lies, tricks, manipulation, and devices that can easily cause you to turn. Do not listen to anything that the enemy says to you. Take all of your commands directly and strictly from God. That is one of the reasons why the Lord wants us to be in direct relationship with Him. Because if you get into a relationship with someone else that wants you to be on their course of life, then you no longer listen to God. The Lord wants you to listen and keep your eyes wide open. It is time to walk in the spirit and see in the spirit.

It is time for people to start being aware of their environment. There are many things happening all around us and we need to be on the watch and in touch with reality. Be watchful, knowing that Jesus Christ will return from the heavens to claim His own people. Be watchful as the elect of God, rebuking the snares of life, set by the enemy. Keep your flesh in subjection to be in the will of God. The will of the flesh is powerful. If you do not put it in subjection by fasting and praying, it will overpower you. Do not allow your flesh and the enemy to bind you. Today, you need to tell the enemy to get under your feet (Romans 16:20, Ephesians 2).

You must also be watchful because the enemy constantly seeks to kill, steal and destroy lives. Hold on to God's unchanging hand. The enemy specializes in trying to manipulate everything he possible can. As soon as you see it happening, start praying because praying puts the devil on the run. Prayer is our direct connection to the one who sits on the throne forever and ever. Call on the name of Jesus because His name makes the enemy flee because there is power in the name. Start counting on Jesus to be the one who helps you in all circumstances. He will make a way out of no way. When you think that you are unable to see the things around you, ask God to open your eyes and make it visible and plain with understanding.

When you start to prosper in your ministry, the enemy will start raising his ugly head in your life, trying to break down or destroy a happy home. We all must be vigilant. No matter what it is, start praying in the Spirit and call on the name of the Lord, Jesus Christ so that the enemy will flee. Rebuke Him entirely. When you know that the enemy has started his attacks, you can start worshipping and singing praises to God to fill the atmosphere. The Holy Spirit will take over. The presence of God will overtake the enemy if you trust Him during your worship and praise sessions.

What do you really want to see? My heart's desire is to see Jesus glorified and serve Him entirely. Your eyes can be opened to see many things in life good or evil.

We want to see a move of God in the lives of His people. We want the word to be revealed to those who have not accepted Christ, according to John 1:1-12. We want them to come back to Jesus. They have lived out in the world long enough. We continue to pray so that they will start pressing their way back in. Ask God to open their eyes by removing the spiritual scales.

A VISION FOR PURPOSE!

Habakkuk 2:2-3 Then the LORD answered me and said: "Write the vision And make *it* plain on tablets, That he may run who reads it. For the vision *is* yet for an appointed time; But at the end it will speak, and it will not lie. Though it tarries, wait for it; Because it will surely come, It will not tarry.

God already set you up for your purpose. He gave you a vision and told you to trust Him. Write the vision and make it plain. You see things that God grants for you as clear as day. Stop refusing the blessing that God has for you. Start speaking it in your spirit that you will be obedient to our Father in heaven. Start confessing with your lips, the promises that God has for you. You do not have to rely on someone else to announce it. Just call on Jesus, the Son of the living God. God will bless your vision especially if it is for His kingdom. If you want it, get it. Blessings are for the taking. Blessings will overflow in what you do for the Lord as long as you glorify Him.

There are many men who built churches for the uplifting of God's kingdom. They are built for worship and praise. King David had a vision to build a temple for God to place the Ark of the Covenant inside. But God wanted a place where He could always dwell. King David could not build the temple because he had blood on his hand. The Temple had to be built by his son, Solomon. You see God has the vision for man. God is looking for those who will be obedient and act on the vision He alone set for them.

When Moses saw the burning bush, his heart was ignited to move toward God. Nevertheless, He moved toward the mountain and discovered it was the voice and the presence of the Lord with a mission for Him. God blessed Moses that day and for days to come. He empowered Moses so that he could tell Pharaoh to let His people go. You see God had a plan for His people. They were to be set free from bondage and be made prosperous all their days.

Jesus had the vision to lay down His life for the world. His vision was to take away the sins of the world. Jesus made it clear that He is the Savior of the world. His vision was to cover everyone in His precious blood. For God so loved the world that He gave His only begotten Son that whosoever believeth in Him shall not perish but have everlasting life. This vision that God has for us is for an appointed time. Jesus' death, burial, and resurrection were for an appointed time. All praise to His holy and righteous name.

You may have to give up something to make you vision happen. You may have to work hard at some things. So be strong in the Lord and in the power of His might. Remember, if the Lord is in it, then it will be successful. Your visions come from God. He is the maker of your inner being and your entire mind. Seek Him for clearer visions. Make your request known to God. You have some visions and dreams inside that must be awakened and manifested to give Him glory.

DON'T LET ANYONE DIVIDE YOUR HOUSE

Matthew 12: 25 But Jesus knew their thoughts, and said to them: Every kingdom divided against itself is brought to desolation, and every city or house divided against itself will not stand.

No man should allow anything to divide his house! He certainly has to be the priest and take full authority before the enemy shows up. The husband and wife should take charge together. Do not destroy your own house because you are not fulfilling your purpose for God and your family. You will be surprised at those who blame other people and the devil. Of course, the enemy always gets a piece when you open up to that mean one.

Nevertheless, do not allow your house to be divided just because you want to have a good time with someone else at the night club or strip joint. Lust will run you out of your mind; force you into adultery and affairs, then out of your house into another person's bed. Take your house back! There is nowhere in the Bible where its states that your house belongs to the devil. So stop giving up to that evil spirit! Put the devil under your feet.

In Ephesians 1:22, Jesus put everything under His feet and was given authority over the church. Conquer your house with God leading the way.. Don't get in God's way. Just ask the Holy Spirit to help you put the enemy under your feet! The writer tells us that "a house divided against itself will not stand." You must keep your house in order because your family is yours for the long haul. Your family is not for the devil's taking. They need the Father's protection and authority! Remain together as husband and wife. Wives, you must be under your husband's covering as well as God's covering. Of course, God is first. Any woman who is not under her husband's covering because of her own pride and ambition will more than likely make herself and family look like fools.

It is extremely important that you do not allow people to divide your relationship with God and your marriage. The man is priest of the home. You are the head of the house so prove it, act like it. Prove your manhood by showing love to your household; prove your manhood by serving Jesus instead of everybody else. Tell your friends that you are a servant of the Most High and that they should serve him in the Spirit! This is when you get your biggest breakthrough! It is because you walk in authority by God's power. No one can take your place because God predestined your future and he intervenes. Your prayers, love, and worship keeps your house together. It's your responsibility to seek the Lord to block the immediate attacks of the enemy.

The goal is to keep holding on to God who is Master over all. Jesus keeps your house together. Be careful not to destroy your own house nor allow anyone else to do it. You set the course in your house under God's mighty hand. You keep the worship flowing in your house. You can ask God to bless and sanctify your home, each day. Give Him thanksgiving from the heart. Remember whose you are, and who you are! You are a child of the Most High God and you will reign with Him in His Kingdom forever. Therefore stop allowing defeat in your house today. Pray now!

What causes a split house or divided house is the failure to love Christ Jesus. It is the failure to communicate, the fear of sound counsel, the lack of trust, and not having the mind of Christ. This is how you allow the enemy to come in and shake up your house.

You have to walk in all of the authority of God because you have Him on your side. Why play with the devil? He already seeks to kill, steal and destroy. In the enemy's eyes, you and I are prey. So when you let your guard down, he loves to come in and wreck your loving home. The enemy wants to make the Lord look bad; but he is a failure and a liar. We know that God is all powerful and has control over that silly enemy.

A happy home filled with love is what you desire. Don't settle for less. You can make love come forth in your home, regardless of the obstacles before you. Every time the enemy puts trip wire in front of you in your house and each room, you will have the ability to walk through and diffuse the situation with the peace of God that surpasses all understanding in your heart and mind. You have an earthen vessel that is filled with power. Also your house is filled with blessings beyond the imagination of all creation including angels and even the enemy. Put your whole armor on and fight back by speaking the word. Tell everyone in your house that you love them. Tell them that Jesus is Lord over this family, over this house.

In Isaiah 9:6, we are told that Jesus is our Counselor. In Proverbs 3:5-6, He said to trust Him. In Roman 12, he admonishes, "be ye transformed by the renewing of your mind". In John 14, He said, "In my house are many mansions, I go to prepare a place for you". It is a blessing to know that the enemy cannot disturb our heavenly house because Jesus lives there. He has blessed us mightily. Keep your house ready for the great day of our Lord's return. Allow the Holy Spirit to run your house. Division is not an option in your house. Run the devil out of your house. Do it by calling on the name of Jesus and praying to our God for help. Pray under the anointing at all times when trouble comes your way. We face the enemy and troubles head on because we are more than conquerors in Christ Jesus. Our confidence is in Him.

Father, you are the peace keeper. You are the reason for living. You are the shelter in storm. You are the one who blesses my house. You are the Priest of my house. I magnify you with all of my heart because of your loving kindness.

OPEN YOUR EYES TO SEE!

Psalm 34:14-20

Depart from evil and do good;
    Seek peace and pursue it.

The eyes of the LORD *are* on the righteous,
    And His ears *are open* to their cry.

**The face of the LORD *is* against those who do evil,
  To cut off the remembrance of them from the earth.**

***The righteous* cry out, and the LORD hears,
  And delivers them out of all their troubles.
The LORD *is* near to those who have a broken heart,
  And saves such as have a contrite spirit.**

**Many *are* the afflictions of the righteous,
  But the LORD delivers him out of them all.
He guards all his bones;
  Not one of them is broken.**

The sight of one bird can amaze us especially when it is going after something it desires. The fact that the eagle can see long distances in the sky and then zero in on a little mouse or other prey is remarkable. It seems like he can see from miles and when he comes in, he moves with precision and skills in a unique attack mode and captures the prey to satisfy that appetite. Why a bird? God chose them to be unique species on earth. This species has remarkable sight and can also spread its wings and go after its prey! God's men and women also have the ability to see as well with Godly precision. We need to use our remarkable sight and pinpoint those that are lost and spread our wings and go and get them! This means you can see in the spirit realm things others may not be able to see. If a donkey can see, surely a human made in the image of God can see in the spirit realm (Numbers 22:28).

We are to open our eyes and see the enemy's attacks and overcome everything he throws at us. God simply desires for His saints to open their eyes and not become prey to the enemy. Turn the tide and call on Jesus to fight your battles. Focus on Jesus, look to Him for help.

God has a specific task for eagles. They help to revolve this ecosystem just like so many other creatures have a purpose in this cycle of life. The scripture says in Isaiah 40:31, "They that wait upon the Lord shall renew their strength; they shall mount up with wings as eagles, they shall run and not be weary, they shall walk, and not faint.

The Bald Eagle demonstrates patience and precision. The eagle also displays zeal to get his prey, food for the baby eaglets.

The mother eagle will not stop until she catches food to feed her children. The eagle has eyes to see hidden prey. When it gets desperate, it seems that the eagle's eye is more powerful than we imagine. The eagle can see from a long distance. This captured my attention because God is always watching us. The Lord our God sees everything straight from heaven. Nothing is able to hide from His presence. He sees all things. He is always on His throne. He never has to leave it. God is present. He comes close to us even faster than the eagle flies. God sends an angel(s) whenever He chooses to help us.. The angels of the Lord fly much faster and are much more powerful. He reminds His saints that His eyes are all on the righteous. Psalm 34:15 the eyes of the LORD *are* on the righteous, And His ears *are open* to their cry. For the righteous, we will be able to see Him like never before. God wants transformed men to open their eyes to see God moving mountains in their lives.

GET READY NOW!

1 CORINTHIANS 15:52 In a moment, in the twinkling of an eye, at the last trumpet. For the trumpet will sound, and the dead will be raised incorruptible, and we shall be changed.

My friend, one moment can make a lifelong difference. One minute can take us directly to God. God is the one who holds all power in His hand. He can do anything. Jesus could return before you can blink an eye. What is this thing called twinkle? In one blink, things could change in your life forever. He could return and take you up in the air. Life happens in a moment. You are here one day, and gone the next day. Have you ever had something in your life affect you so fast before you could know it was coming? This is important because there are people who do not understand that their heart is beating because God allows it to beat. If He took away a few heart beats you would feel a difference. We expect the last trumpet to sound so that we will rise incorruptible and be changed in the twinkling of an eye. We are the people of the Lord and He will not go back on His word. Listen to what the Lord is saying. A change is coming and everyone needs to get ready for the blessed return of the Lord. You do not want to miss him when He comes back.

THE GOODNESS OF GOD!

EXODUS 33:18-20 And he said, please show me your glory. Then He said I will make all My goodness pass before you, and I will proclaim the name of the Lord before you. I will be gracious to whom I will be gracious, I will have compassion on whom I will have compassion. But He said, you cannot see my face; For no man shall see Me, and live.

God is good all of the time. His goodness extends throughout our lives. If we are His people, we can just walk in the goodness of God. The goodness is within God's glory. The goodness of God is in His presence and power pouring out in your life right now, and extends throughout eternity. As long as you can take a breath and live this life, it is the goodness of God. His goodness is eternal.

We respond to His goodness and glory when we praise and worship Him. Moses got a glimpse of God passing in His own glory. This had to be the most powerful moment in Moses' life. God took out time to show Himself to Moses, one who was once a murderer, but now a deliverer. This is the same God who spoke the universe into existence. Somehow the God of the universe walked in His own manifested glory to reveal to Moses that He is God. He did not have to do it. He did it because of His love, purpose and plan for Israel. Moses did not work in vain. God made a statement that no other God could do. There is nothing to which we can compare the glory of God. He expressed His love, power and presence. He reveals His compassion.

Listen to what God said, "I will make my goodness pass before you. Has anyone ever said they had a Goodness that would bless you and be gracious to no? No, absolutely not. The only one who could pass before you and show His glory is God.

I believe that God is showing us that He passes before us on so many occasions, but we miss His presence. He passes before us in the midnight hour when no one else is there to see Him but You and His Holy Angels. He passes before us when we are in hurting situations and it seems like there is no shoulder to cry on. He wipes the tears away. He passes before us when trouble comes our way and it seem like the enemy may have the victory. But God passes by and steps right in the situation and turns it around. He is good. His mercy endureth forever. When God shows His presence to you, there must be something on His mind. He desires to bless you, mold you, and strengthen you for a journey that seems to be endless. He puts some of His on glory on you and makes everything alright. He will never pass by and not bless you. God is always up to something. Moses knew it, that is why Moses said, "Show me your glory".

And this is how we pray, "Show me your glory in the midnight hour when I need you to touch me. Show me your glory when life seems too hard to bear. God, I need you to talk to me. Speak your word through your manifested glory."

CHAPTER 2
A CONNECTION TO GOD

JOHN 15:7 If you abide in Me, and My words abide in you, you will ask what you desire, and it shall be done for you.

You know when you have a strong connection to God; you will trust him in everything and watch the manifestation of his power in your life. Listen, if you abide in Him, you will have favor. The word abide means to remain, to stay, to persevere, to remain in him, and to be true. God wants each Christian to remain in him. Stay connected to God so he can be your power source.

Jesus reveals to us in John 15 that we need to abide in Him. He is referring to following Jesus Christ (Christianity). There is no other way around it. The Bible declares that He is the truth, the way and life. There is no other way to the Father, but by Him. He does not mention anything about abiding in another religion outside of Himself. One can only follow Jesus Christ. There is only one true and wise God. Anything dealing with the flesh does not abide in Jesus Christ. We must be totally connected to Jesus. You cannot be connected to a second god. Jesus teaches us about the truth of His promises. He will answer our petition if we stick with Him instead of the skeptics. He made it simple to all believers. "If you abide in me, and my words abide in you, you will ask what you desire, and it shall be done for you." He wants us to know Him. He wants to know if you trust Him totally with His word. Understand that our God owns everything in this world and the worlds to come. In Proverbs, He said, "If you delight yourself in Him, He will give you the desires of your heart." Make your desire to be transformed into a new creature in Jesus Christ. Ask Jesus to help you to abide in Him to help you walk this Christian walk so that you can bless other people.

He is the Creator and can make anything possible that seems impossible. He is the God of the invisible who makes things come to be. So when you are looking at impossibilities, God is up to something in your life. He will turn it around. Take a look right now at your life. Our Father in Heaven is capable of supplying all of our needs. According to Philippians 4:19, "And my God shall supply all your needs according to His riches in glory by Christ Jesus." We have the word that gives us access to all of God's solutions and blessings. Thank God that we have His supernatural power. The Lord shows supernatural results. He can give you the healing you want. Abide in Him, and allow His word to abide in you, and then ask Him to lead you on this journey. He can visit any hospital and demonstrate His power in miracles. He can raise someone from the sick bed when death approaches. He is the God of resurrection and miracles. There are witnesses to His power. You can read 1 Corinthians 15. People saw the dead walking the streets because of his resurrection power. I am telling you today that if you want the promises of God, abide in Him and let His word abide in you, then ask what you desire. He is the God of resurrection power.

God is the answer to all of our hopes, dreams and desires. He can and will fulfill what is necessary in our lives according to His word and purpose. We can count on God to bless us in so many ways. He is blessing us right this very minute. If you are alive, He is blessing you. The same God in Heaven sent us the Holy Spirit to guide us for the purpose of glorifying Him in our lives. We need a consistent prayer life to keep our lines of communication open to God and to maintain our obedience and humility toward Him. That is exactly why He gave us the Holy Spirit. In Romans 8:26-28, God sent the Holy Spirit to make intercession for us, especially in our weakness. He knows exactly what you and I need.

Believers know that God has the power to control everything from His throne in Heaven. I like the attitude that Peter and John had in Acts 3, when they saw the lame man at the gate Beautiful. A miracle happened when Peter said in Act 3:6 "Silver and gold I do not have, But what I do have I give you, In the name of Jesus Christ of Nazareth, rise up and walk." According to scripture, that lame man got up leaping and walking and rejoicing. This man had been there for a while expecting something to happen sooner or later; and it did. God blessed Him. Today you can get up and walk out of your lame condition.

WITNESS AND TESTIFY

1 CORINTHIANS 15:3-6 For I delivered to you first of all that which I also received: That Christ died for our sins according to the scripture, and that He was buried and that He rose again on the third day according to the scripture, and that He was seen by Cephas, then by the twelve. After that He was seen by five hundred brethren at once, of whom the greater part remain to the present, but some have fallen asleep.

Make sure you become an effective witness. Be equipped in the word of God. Study to show yourself approved a workman rightly dividing the word. You can win somebody! Your attitude and respect for others goes a long way. Just think, because you are the kind of person that loves people, you get to win people to the Lord. I see it at our Church, Christian Worship Center often, when our women bring people to church on Sundays. It is the love you have for our Savoir, Jesus that will push you into winning somebody to Christ. This is your winning season. Take advantage! Because you have experienced something in Jesus Christ, you have evidence that He lives. Be a witness from this day on. You can make history when you tell someone of how powerful Jesus is.

If you recall in John 1:1-8, He had come to His own and they received Him not and that was in the beginning. Jesus already knew that people were going to reject Him. Pilate rejected the fact that He was the Messiah, Christ in the flesh. Pilate, if you recall, did not want to dirty his hands. But he still turned the Lord over to the mob.

I thank God that He allowed this vessel to use this scripture today with a brother who wants to get back into a relationship with the Lord. The Lord will always have a witness. He will never run out - no matter what happens. Somebody is going to have to tell of His resurrection. Somebody will have to tell of His saving grace. You can never get away with the most elementary facts of Jesus. Christ died for our sins. Secondly, He was buried and raised from the dead on the third day. It is amazing in God's plan that He could strategically place people to see Him and turn over some of the

27

blessings. Five hundred people had seen Jesus after His resurrection. Then there were 12 disciples that saw Him.

A MAN ROOTED IN JESUS CHRIST1

Ephesians 3:17-19 that Christ may dwell in your hearts through faith; that you, being rooted and grounded in all love, may be able to comprehend with all the saints what is the width, the length and depth and height- to know the love of Christ which passes knowledge; that you may be filled with all fullness of God.

My friend, the Lord wants every man and woman to be rooted in Jesus Christ. This will throw the adversary off track! A root is normally associated with a plant or a tree. In most cases, the root runs deep in the ground. The roots run with strength and power and are anchored with power. Psalms 1 tells us about being rooted by the rivers of the water to receive continuous nourishment that never ends. When you are rooted in Jesus, all power is accessible to you, in you and for you. The power you get runs even stronger and with more nourishment than the rivers of water that nourish the roots. You belong to God, so allow him to be rooted in you so that you can reflect his image. You will reflect the power of God's image and glory around others.

You need the kind of faith that connects and anchor you to Jesus. The word of God roots you. Keep reading the word so your faith will be stronger as well. You need real faith to know that you are rooted in Christ. If a minister, deacon or any church member falls from the faith because of some sinful act, they should be rooted in Jesus enough to seek repentance sincerely and get back into proper position in Jesus Christ. Don't let the devil take you from Jesus Christ. Remember that you belong to Jesus Christ. You are connected to the fullness of God. Stop acting, walking and looking defeated. Hold your head up and call on Jesus in the time of need. Make no mistake, you do need Him! You can act like you are so intellectual if you want, God will knock you to your knees or he will allow the devil to do it. All he has to do is remove his hand off of your life. That is not what you want to happen. Ask Jesus to keep his hand on your life.

What do you think the Apostle Paul was saying to the church? Surely He was encouraging them to know that fullness of blessings are in the Lord, Jesus Christ. He was praying for the believers in the church at Ephesus that they would be strengthened in the inner man. He was encouraging them to hold on to Jesus Christ, who sanctifies us, roots and grounds us in the faith through our hearts. He knows that your heart must be rooted and grounded in Him in order to make it through the rough times of life and even the tribulation period. He knows that your heart is a vessel for His spirit to flow through and speak to for His purpose. He knows to use you right now because your faith is in Him.

There will be some hard and evil things that will approach you in life in the natural and in the spirit. But our precious Savior knows how to rescue us and comfort us all at the same time. He has that kind of power. We, as saints, must walk with the fullness of God in our hearts. I am finding out every day that there are challenges that await us before we even wake up good. We need the fullness of God to dwell in our hearts even to forgive anyone who comes up against us with evil plots and schemes and dysfunctional attitudes and behaviors. It takes the love of God in your heart and that means the fullness of Him to overcome and forgive on a daily basis.

The Apostle Paul said that we "may be able to comprehend with all the saints what is the width, the length and depth and height –to know the love of Christ which passes knowledge; that you may be filled with all the fullness of God." He took my mind back to High School when we had to work out mathematics with a similar type of equations. God is not an equation. He is not complicated. He is the God of multiple blessings and I believe that is why we cannot comprehend the width, length, and depth of His unfailing love. His love is so powerful that it fills the very core of all of our being to keep us in His perfect will.

If you are challenged by anything in your life, if you are lonely, feel abandoned or have medical complications, or maintaining your faith, please understand that there is nothing more powerful than His love. Put away fornication and pornography. You are better than that! Don't let the enemy set you up for a sexual disease. Take authority over your life. Don't let anyone put you down. You are just as good as anyone else in this world! If anyone tries to put you down, it is a lie from the devil. Rebuke it and get on with God's blessings in your life. You are never alone. He will never leave you nor forsake you. He knows all about your decision to kick the drug habit, put down the alcohol, and leave the world of sin.

Today cast down every bondage that has been trying to destroy you. Today, ask God to cast down evil imaginations and strongholds that are keeping you from allowing Jesus to come into your heart. If you did not do it, it is because you are allowing the devil to rule your life. Do not accept that evil voice. Call Jesus name at least seven times.

Repeat this In Jesus name, I am clean, In Jesus name, I am made whole, in Jesus name, My life is worth living, In Jesus name, I am rich in my inheritance! In Jesus name, all my bad habits are over. I am a new creature in Christ Jesus.

Lord Jesus I repent of my sin today! Jesus, I believe and I confess that you are the Son of God and that you died for my sins and on the third day you rose from the dead with all power in your hand by the Father in heaven. Come into my heart. I accept you as Lord in my life from this day on. May all praise, glory and honor go to your name O' Lord.

DELIVERED THROUGH BONDAGE

ROMANS 6:6 Knowing this, that our old man was crucified with Him, that the body of sin might be done away with, that we should no longer be slaves of sin.

UNBROKEN MIND!

An unbroken mind symbolizes that you have discovered your identity and have not allowed the enemy to rule over your mind, soul and spirit. An unbroken mind is someone with healthy thoughts. This person trust in God and knows how to get on with their life regardless of those that hate on you, disrespect, put you down, never compliment you or lift you up and those that turn their back on you. Thank God that He gave me an unbroken mind to depend on Him. The reflection of an unbroken mind is Jesus in your life. If there is no Jesus in your life, then you are already broken by the enemy. Don't be fooled! Ask yourself if you are living an undercover life of sin. You know what it means. You are doing things that you think no one else can see, especially in the dark. The devil has your life in his hand if you have not accepted Jesus as Lord in your life.

If it is not Sunday and you are reading this, you need to get on your knees and ask Jesus to come into your heart because you are being set up by the devil for a great fall and you will impact your family. You need to be strong enough as the man of the house or the woman of the house to lift your family up, especially those that walk around defeated. You have a chance to get that other person and yourself to a church that preaches sound doctrine of Jesus Christ. Then get baptized after you accept Jesus in your heart. Move faster and stop thinking about it. Just do it! If you get close to Jesus, you have a chance because the victory is in Jesus Christ, the Anointed One and Son of the Living God. Don't be enslaved to the devil and his demons. Come out of darkness! It can be daylight but you can still be in darkness. You need to know where you stand. You need to know that you came out of darkness and are now walking in the light! Praise the Lord!

One example of darkness is continuing in sexual affairs or sexual misbehavior with the soldier or man who **is at war in** Afghanistan or Iraq. You shouldn't be involved in bi- sexual behavior with anyone. But you need to know that you are in darkness and this applies to believers, non-believers, Christians, Muslims or any religion. You need to come out of darkness and serve Jesus Christ. The woman needs to repent who is committing adultery with a man and about to become pregnant or already is while her husband is in war serving his country. You see the devil does not care who you are. You can be perfectly happy in your marriage and the enemy comes in like a storm and rips it apart, devastating your life. You need Jesus. Stop playing games. Stop playing with fire, stop mingling with evil spirits. Stop throwing your life and relationship down the drain for a few feel good moments. You need a relationship with Jesus Christ today!

God's people, living in Egypt, were in bondage, traps, forced slavery by Pharaoh and his taskmasters. I wonder how many thought about breaking free vs those who were so entrenched into slavery that it was the only thing they could see and think in their minds. That is not what God wanted and He proved it. That is not what God desires for us today. He wants each of us to be free! God wants our minds to be unbroken. He wants our minds to be clear of a slavery mentality from the enemy. He wants His children to know that they are free in Jesus Christ! Do you know that you are free? Do you want to walk in freedom? When I first saw the series, Roots and how bad slaves were treated and their desire to be free, it caused tears to flow. It was hard to even think that one man could possibly treat another man in such a dehumanized way. Slaves fought back for freedom and many people in slavery worshipped and prayed to our Father in Heaven to intervene and set them free. God heard their cry and delivered African Americans from bondage just as He did with the children of Israel. Slave masters held men on plantations for years against their own will and whipped them to prove their dominance and power. But God our Father took charge of the situation and set African Americans free. Likewise Jesus set men free from the power of sin's grip and those affected areas where sin tapped into and had taken root. Jesus took us from the power of sin into His power of grace and love. Tell all enemies that try to have a grip on you to let you go! You can break through all bondages and drop all baggage at the door-outside.

We must know that all our sin was taken away in the death of Jesus Christ on the cross. The crucifixion was one of the worst forms of execution. Jesus was crucified for the world. He hung on a cross and his body carried the sin of everyone on planet earth. He was nailed to the cross and could not get down because Jesus was on a mission to please His Father in saving the world.

The crucifixion caused Jesus and the other criminals to lose body fluids. It is the weight of the victim that causes death. Jesus wore thorns that were put on His head. He experienced a spear that pierced His side causing blood to come streaming out of His body. He died because He bore the sins of the world resulting in defeat of the enemy and destroying sin's power once and for all. His crucifixion stood for eternal love, joy and peace. His blood washed away my sin and yours. The next time you take a hard look at your body, understand that Jesus' took our place on the cross. We deserved wrath not Him. It was and still is His everlasting love that saved us from God's wrath.

We are asked to crucify our flesh that we can walk in the Spirit. We are not strong enough to walk alone. We need our Father in heaven, the Holy Spirit to strengthen us in our Christian walk. Our lives are not ours. We belong to Jesus now. We believe in Jesus Christ as the son of God. We were created for God's purpose. He wants us to crucify this flesh so that we will be under his subjection and will. The tendency in life is to worship the wrong god, without even realizing the danger of it. The reason why we need to cast off some things in our lives is because Jesus already destroyed the power of sin and made us free. Listen to what the Apostle Paul said, we should no longer be slaves of sin. We do not need to get in these comfort zones where we accept any old thing. We should avoid things such as the Buddhist prayer, temples, false gods, and religions that believe and welcome sin. These things cause us to become slaves all over again.

To be crucified with Jesus means to put off the old you and clothe yourself in righteousness. You have to be reminded that you are a new creature in Christ; the old man has passed away. Old things have to be broken like unhealthy sexual relationships, alcoholism drug use and bad habits that involve sin. .

If you need to go on a diet, you can crucify the flesh. The Apostle Paul said in Philippians 3:10 "that I may know Him and the power of His resurrection, and the fellowship of His sufferings, being conformed to His death," Get your sights set on Him and know Him. He is the only true and wise God. He is the redeemer of my soul and yours.

You can start anytime walking as a saint. It is a good thing to acknowledge who you are in Christ and allow your light to shine and your flesh to be crucified. Start walking in the ministry as a new creature and new man in Christ. Jesus will not let you go. There are blessings in your walk with Jesus Christ. You can walk in boldness and power. The blessings come because of your obedience. What kind of blessings? You name it, God will supply. Let everyone know who ask that you are a child of the King of Glory and He will not let you down.

WALK IN NEW LIFE!

ROMANS 6:4 Therefore we were buried with Him through baptism into death, that just as Christ was raised from the dead by the glory of the Father, even so we should also walk in the newness of life.

You can have a new life in Jesus Christ any time you want it. It is available twenty four-seven, anytime you call on Him. The good thing about it is that you do not have to beg for it; just surrender. Become a transformed man and walk in your new life. When He transforms you, you will walk with power and authority. God already knows your heart's desire. Walk in newness of life and never look back. He already knows whether you trust Him or not. If you trust Him, He will bless you. You need to confess that you believe in Him then allow Jesus to come into your heart right now. Once you do it, you will be transformed right before everyone.

In baptism, a person is immersed into the water who has committed their lives to our Lord, Jesus Christ. The person goes down into the water and comes up symbolic of the resurrection of Jesus from the dead, meaning his death signified all sin was destroyed. When He rose from the grave it meant new life and authority and the grip of Satan could no longer enslave you or keep you in his prison of hell. In other words, the old person is left in the water and the new person will rise to walk with Christ. Do you want to walk in Jesus Christ today? Then fulfill his commands. In Matthew 28, Jesus states, be baptized in the name of the Father, of the Son, and the Holy Ghost.

I never liked visiting graveyards because there was death all around. And it sends off an uncomfortable feeling. But I realize now that I am dead to sin and alive in Christ. So my life and thought process are different. I am no longer who I use to be. I am a new creature in Christ Jesus. The graveyard now only symbolizes that time is up; a new life must start in the spirit. The past life is gone. The old man is dead and gone and buried.

It is interesting that the Father raised Jesus up. Sometimes people do not want to hear that. However, they need to hear it. They need to witness what God has done for His people.

A FATHER'S HEART

LUKE 15:15-23 Then he went and joined himself to a citizen of that country, and he sent him into his fields to feed swine. And he would gladly have filled his stomach with the pods that the swine ate, and no one gave him *anything*. "But when he came to himself, he said, 'How many of my father's hired servants have bread enough and to spare, and I perish with hunger! I will arise and go to my father, and will say to him, "Father, I have sinned against heaven and before you, and I am no longer worthy to be called your son. Make me like one of your hired servants."' "And he arose and came to his father. But when he was still a great way off, his father saw him and had compassion, and ran and fell on his neck and kissed him. And the son said to him, 'Father, I have sinned against heaven and in your sight, and am no longer worthy to be called your son.' "But the father said to his servants, 'Bring[1] out the best robe and put *it* on him, and put a ring on his hand and sandals on *his* feet. And bring the fatted calf here and kill *it*, and let us eat and be merry

If you want to see a display of a Father's heart, look at God. He looked at His son who was on the cross and turned away from Him because of sin, so that He could be crucified. Then God, the Father, turned right back around and raised His beloved Son Jesus from the dead and took Him out of the grave.

Take a look at the Prodigal Son's father who blessed him upon his return home after the son had been disobedient, because greed filled his heart. The father took him back into the house and blessed him. The Prodigal's father demonstrated a true father's heart when he accepted him, instead of turning him away. It is the Father who teaches the son survival skills. Those skills are taught so that he can rely on God, and then glorify our Father in heaven. We need our Father in heaven. He loves us so much that he sent the Holy Ghost to work through us and help us.

Most sons are ambitious, especially when they meet someone who is strong. They have the same desire to achieve. But when they cry for help, it is a different sound. God makes known to you the blessing that awaits. Men you are to be aware of when you need to step in and nurture that young son, regardless if he is a blood son or step-son. Step in and step up. I discovered that my son was listening, but not hearing. Sometimes he's hearing but not listening. In other words, nothing effective is happening.

My father was my hero in my life. He took care of 7 children and then his brothers and sisters. He took care of more than of what he was obligated. He was just a young adult, but his heart led him to bless others. God fixed it where fathers have to know when to love and when to keep things in high intensity. Men like the Prodigal son need to learn the lesson that you cannot get over the father in your house. Every young man and daughter needs to rely on the wisdom of their father. If they ignore the wisdom, then all types of confusion could be the results. In other words, God speaks to your father and He speaks to you as well. One thing you have to understand is authority and who God orders in your house.

One of the most powerful things that can happen in the house is when a Father forgives and grants a kiss. He may not have to kiss, as the Prodigal Son's father. But if he forgives sincerely, God has smiled on him.

Today take hold of the word of God. Take hold of the God who has redeemed us from the devil's grip. Jesus spoke of His Father in prayer. Let us pray like Jesus did. Jesus said, "Our Father in heaven, Hallowed be Your name, Your Kingdom come. Your will be done. On earth as it is in heaven. Give us this day our daily bread. And forgive our debts, As we forgive our debtors. And do not lead us into temptation, But deliver us from the evil one. For yours is the kingdom and the power and the glory forever. Amen Matthew 6.

A HEART WITHOUT FEAR

HEBREWS 13:5-6 Let your conduct be without covetousness; be content with such things as you have. For He Himself has said, "I will never leave you nor forsake you." So we may boldly say: "The LORD is my helper; I will not fear. What can man do to me?

Surely no one should have a covetous spirit. God desires that we are content with what He provides. However, we should never be content when it does not meet the Lord's standard. We have to know that the Lord will help us in any situation according to His will only.

When it comes to fear, our natural instinct or reaction in the presence of a lion would be to run. The lion does not show fear in most cases. He shows the opposite, strength and power. Likewise the bear and the elephant will not show fear. You can find that the serpent will strike at you and make you think fear. Fight back like a lion who does not back down.

From another view, there is always something going on in this world that need some attention. You may need to give tough love or just plain old roughing-them-up kind of love. We administered the latter to the soldiers in the armed forces.. One of the phrases my friend, Willie, use to use all the time at work regarding soldiers is "Scuff Him Up" we got some laughs on that one phrase. The phrase was used toward soldiers who had no discipline, mostly new recruits just coming in or a soldier who wouldn't follow orders. In those days, you could tell a Private First Class to pay attention to detail in conducting a simple packing list, he would do the very opposite, even after instructions. He had to be taught, shown instructions, and then put to the test. That simple packing list could means the difference in life or death. There were also times when soldiers needed to drop and push up. We would assign or have them "knock them out" 100-200 push-ups to get them physically in shape. This would also stimulate and condition their minds to motivate them to respond and meet standards. This was to make a better soldier ready for combat. There were times when the Drill Sergeant would have to get the Senior Drill Sergeant to get involved. The Senior Drill Sergeant already had in his mind to drop the soldiers and keep them learning discipline and readiness. It was also to make them strong and to overcome fear in combat. If they learned the standards and developed discipline, fear would not be an option. Although it may come, but a soldier once engaged, could overcome it when he fights back.

Gang violence is also on the rise in so many areas in our communities. It seems that it never ceases. Innocent people are always victims of unnecessary violence. You can visit almost any country and find out that someone needs help against predators. Sin is like a predator that keeps on seeking who it can take hold of and destroy. You need the word for your protection. This is what you need to do, speak the word, so you can rough that enemy up. Instead of you being on the end of receiving the blow, you shake the enemy up with the word. You do not have to be victimized any more. Tell the enemy that God's word has you and you are content in His word. It's powerful and cuts through every attack of the enemy and demons in his army.

You have the victory so start walking in it. That will affect him. Stop the enemy under your feet. Saints, it is time to get together and rough him up. Start praying saints. Make time to pray today, right now in Jesus' name. Pray until you have a breakthrough. Pray until you hear from God. When you pray, please understand that the enemy is receiving a blow to the head each and every time. It is time for you to believe that the power of the Lord is at work in your life. When we pray, we pray expecting something to happen and honoring God at the same time.

You do not have to worry about being afraid again. The Lord said that He will never leave you nor forsake you. I am content with the blessings of the Lord. Even
Though I am content with blessings flowing in my life, I still have a mission to witness and serve Him.

There is no need of counting me out of the picture. That is the attitude all of us need to gain. You see in my witness and my service, God is always there. That is exactly how I know it's time to rough the devil up. It makes no sense if the enemy keeps attacking you and you do nothing but entertain Him over and over again. Some people walk around moping and crying about what the enemy did to them. All they have to do is to use the faith power with which God has equipped them.   It is time to live like you are ready to rough the enemy up. If you were in the combat zone, you would put full force and full ammunition to the targeted enemy. Use your prayers. Give God all the glory.

GOD ORDAINED YOU!

JEREMIAH 1:5 "Before I formed you in the womb I knew you; Before you were born I sanctified you; I ordained you a prophet to the nations."

You had a destiny before you were even born! God already knew you! What does that tell you? He still knows you by name. You did not get lost from Jesus. He still sees you. You may have broken relationship with Him. Today you can come back right now! You need to break relationship with anything evil. The devil thinks he owns you. You need to speak the word. You need to confess that Jesus sanctified you in your mother's womb and you belong to Jesus. Tell that enemy you are one of Jesus' ordained prophets to speak the word, so the enemy will flee.

The Lord, God knew everything before it happened to you and me. God knew you had a call in your life. He called you like Jesus Christ did. God told Jeremiah that I knew you before you were in your mother's womb. How can you know someone before the seed had even been developed? God is the one who decides what the seed will be; because He made the seed in man. We existed in God's eyes even before our time could be manifested on earth. That is a reason to shout because no one else can express such power and make creative miracles come into existence.

God wanted Jeremiah to be encouraged about his mission. Jeremiah was appointed by God as His prophet to the nations. He wanted Jeremiah to know that all power is in His hand and that He would be with Him in delivering His messages. So to express His power, He told Jeremiah that He knew him before He was even conceived.

The Lord has already thought about us before we could even know ourselves, before we even came into the world. He knew everything about each person individually and accurately before we could know anything about ourselves. That is enough to shout about. God knew our hearts, minds, soul, and strength before we knew anything about it. What a reason to praise Him and serve Him the rest of your life!

Everyone that God calls has a specific purpose. No one should live life without knowing their purpose. If you do not know, ask God. Seek Him with all of your heart and soul and He will answer. The word of God is also the answer. God will bless you through His word. Seek ye first the kingdom of God and His righteousness. When you seek Him everything else that He desires for you will follow and bless you.

There are several things that God wants you to do and more. You may not finish everything; but set goals in Christ Jesus. Jesus can help you make it through all of your goals. He made you and me before time. He already had us in mind before the world was formed. Not only did He already know us, He sanctified you. He ordains the person He wants to ordain for His purpose. God has a mission for His people. He set apart specific people for pinpointed assignments. Moses is an example. His assignment was to lead God's people out of Egypt, from slavery. God used him to set his people free. Moses was known as a deliverer chosen by God (Exodus 13:17-14:31). Do you know your assignment? Do you know where God wants you? Remember, before He formed you and me, He already knew about us. He knew everything about us. He knew our comprehension levels, he knew our intellect, and He knew who we would marry. He knew the trust level inside our hearts. He knew if we would accept Him as Lord and Savior. He knew that He would wash us in His blood for the remission of sins. He knew who would give birth to a baby boy or girl. He knew those who would have twins, triplets and even quadruplets. God knew the morning and the days of the year and times of thunder and lighting and the floods of life. He knew how much trouble we would face. He knew and knows it all.

GOD GAVE YOU A MISSION BROTHER!

The Apostle Paul's Four Missionary journeys,

To be a man on a mission for God, you must be ready to face some demons, giants and some people that will throw arrows at you and try to push you off course. You just need to get the seed in you, which is the word of God to equip you and allow God to use you. You also have to be willing and obedient in putting time and effort into the mission for God. Go on the mission that the Lord had been calling you to do for the last 10-20 years. You just sat there and thought God had forgotten. He has not forgotten. He still knows who you are. Make no mistake. He will convert you, equip and empower you to get the mission done. He will also supply what you need in abundance. The Apostle Paul expressed an attitude of belief and surrender to Christ by going on four missionary journeys in an effort to reach out to all Christians, churches and the lost that he may win souls to the Kingdom of God. He wanted to make an impact to please God, our Father in heaven. What a thought? Do you want to please our Father in heaven when he asks you to do one thing in your life?

When God asks you to go out and touch someone's life, it is because you are in His plan as well as the multitude of people that he wants you to reach. All believers know that God has the power to control everything from heaven and any place He wants to control. He owns an operation center everywhere, in every country and in every nation.   The Lord's presence is in your vessel as well as in every house of God, the Church. No one can stop Him from controlling all things. Since Jesus has power over all things such as the sky, land, hilltops, valleys, streams, rivers, oceans, men, women, and children. The spiritual realm, life on earth, death, and eternal life and all things are under His authority. So surely he can watch over you while you are on your mission overseas or near home. Make no mistake, the Apostle knew that the Holy Spirit was leading his life. Whatever you do for God, ask the Holy Spirit to lead you on that mission.

BREAK YOUR STRONGHOLD & TRAPS!

2 Corinthians 10:4- 5 For the weapons of our warfare are not carnal, but mighty through God to the pulling down of strong holds; Casting down imaginations, and every high thing that exalteth itself against the knowledge of God, and bringing into captivity every thought to the obedience of Christ;

The Apostle Paul breached the lines of the enemy with the power of the Holy Spirit as he went on journey after journey to tell somebody about Jesus Christ and His miracle working power. The Apostle Paul had the audacity and the boldness to venture out and position himself where God wanted to use him. He was led by the Holy Spirit to be an evangelist and missionary in the field by touching thousands of lives. He was led by the Holy Spirit to breach all lines of the enemy including booby traps laid for him. His goal was to press for the prize and glorify Jesus Christ. The Apostle Paul wanted to be pleasing in God's sight. The Apostle wanted people to also know that our weapons are mighty through God and will enable us to pull down every stronghold in your life and mine.

It was Jesus who blessed the Apostle Paul to become the saint he turned out to be. I think what was important is that God placed His word in this vessel and used Him mightily. He was an instrument for Jesus Christ and the word of God was his weapon to use against the enemy. This meant also that a relationship and prayer would help pull down every stronghold.

It was the Apostle who expounded on the word Grace. In Ephesians 2:8 He reminds us that all enemy lines are breached. The devil's camp has been infiltrated so saints can win back lost brothers and sisters. We have a God that is so powerful and mighty who gave us grace, a gift that the enemy can't touch. Grace can't be altered. Grace can't be shattered. Grace can't be manipulated. Grace can't be stolen or lost. Grace can't be taken away. God owns it and allows us to preach His word so it will not return void. Grace is able to break through every obstacle of the enemy and man's bondage and fleshly desires. God is good and worthy of all praise. That is exactly why you and I can rest in His grace. No need to worry about anything. We have grace on our side and Jesus to back it up.

In the military, it takes professionalism and training and discipline to spot those booby traps and the enemy IEDs, and those around the corner aiming RPGs and missiles to take on casualties. We have grace to keep us in His perfect will. When you are in battle, it is because you either accepted Jesus as Lord or you are living a lifestyle that pleases the devil. The Lord desires you to walk as a new creature in Jesus Christ and a warrior.

We are so blessed because God showers us in grace. You see because we stay soaked in grace by the spiritual rain of blessings from God, we can breach anything in life. If there is a challenge in marriage, you can breach the troubles because you have grace and you have a high Priest who has already blessed you.

Grace gives you the will to survive in any and every situation. Grace carries you to the edge and back. It takes you through all enemy attacks. Grace enables you to grow. It took Jesus to breach all lines of the enemy. Adam could not do it because he had sinned with his wife. All of the old prophets and Jesus disciples could not do it. It took the blood of Jesus to breach the most fortified and built up area of hell.

The need to minister involves grace. The Lord will prepare all of those like Apostle Paul to run the mission outside. There is always a need for God's ministry. God put His ministry in place. When one falls, then one who lives for the purpose of Christ and His marvelous presence is raised up. You are one or the other. Do not allow circumstances and other people to get in your way. Seek God and ask Him for direction and purpose for your life. God is always looking for new journeymen like you. He is looking for journey women also. He has a way of sending His anointing through those who seek Him and love Him with an open heart of thanksgiving.

GLORIFY HIS NAME!

PSALM 8:1 O LORD, Our LORD, how excellent is your name in all the earth, who have set Your Glory above the heavens!

God's name alone has all power to shake kingdoms, shape kingdoms, and loose those that are bound by the grip of the enemy. His name alone declares His glory and strength. His name is the highest name there is throughout creation. Jesus is Lord, anyway we look at it. His name is excellent because there is no one like Him and His glory is revealed throughout the ages. His name is above the heavens because He is the creator of all things including the stars, planets, moon, earth, and even death and life. He makes the impossible possible. Imagine in your mind that God designed the man with His soul and spirit. All people and everything must bow before Him in full worship. He is excellent, glorious and worthy of all praise. The Lord is recognized. He is forever merciful and all loving.

Our Lord is the one who is responsible for putting a soul inside of man. He is responsible for putting a spirit inside of man. The scriptures say, that "He breathed the breath of life into man and man became a living soul." In that process, we became His alone. That is why men must bow before Him in adoration. I believe the excellence of the Lord's name was etched into the minds of men even before they accepted Him. With God's name, everything has a touch of holiness. Man must glorify Him for what He has done and is performing right now in the life of the believer and even in the natural man.

BELIEVE IN JESUS

John 20:27-29 Then He said to Thomas, Reach your finger here, and look at My hands; And reach your hand here, and put it into My side. Do not be unbelieving, but believing, And Thomas answered and said to Him, My Lord and My God! Jesus said Thomas because you have seen me, you have believed. Blessed are those who have not seen and yet believed.

Become a believer today while it is not too late! The Bible

illustrates several times that Jesus touched people in different situations. What was so important about His touch is that He always made it personal. Healing was a result of His touch. It was His love that restored us. His love touched our lives so that we could believe and be focused on Him. He touched the blind, He touched the lame, He touched those with Leprosy, He touched those tortured by demons, and influenced by witches. He touched broken men and women. He even touched the dead. He allowed the hem of His garment to be touched by a woman with a blood issue. Jesus never turns us away from His love. His unfailing love, grace, mercy and healing power is for all people. He can touch anybody He wants. God desires to touch each one of us, every day. God is in control of life. Believe in Him! Believe in Him and receive all the blessings you have been refusing or blocking.

You might have a personal experience one day that binds you to something out of God's will. But God will deliver you from those issues because you are one of His and He knows that you trust in Him.

It was hard for Thomas for a little while, but he came around and believed in Jesus after He had risen from the dead. Thomas' faith grew instantly. He believed in the resurrection. He believed that Jesus is the son of God.

The blind man wanted to see and he finally found someone who could change the course of his life. When you ask the Lord for sight, you might as well trust Him because it will happen. Your old spiritual scales will fall off. Your eyes will be opened for the first time. Strange things can happen for the first in the life of the believer. Your life could be different from that blind man's experience. God might have you doing a great work to glorify Him. So He needs you to see in the spirit.

The woman with the issue of blood just wanted to touch the hem of His garment. Her faith was noticed by Jesus. Jesus asked "Who touched me?" because He knew that someone had touched Him in faith. So He spoke to her, "Your faith has made you whole." God wants us to have that kind of faith to know that He will make us whole. Even if the physicians can not heal you, the Lord will make you whole again. You just need to ask Him to touch your situation, no matter what it is; He has the power to change it.

The men with leprosy had more than they could handle. They saw Jesus and asked for healing. They knew that they were outcasts. They knew that their conditions were contagious and had to be controlled or else it would spread. But when they saw Jesus, they knew that all they had to do was ask for healing. Jesus healed them and one of them praised Him and rejoiced for His mighty act. You may have felt like an outcast because of a medical issue or because life just dealt you a blow. Call on the name of the Lord. He is our strong tower. He is our healer.

What was amazing is the fact that when Jesus rose from the dead, he did not want to be touched by Mary, because as He said, "I am not ascended yet into heaven". Yet he ate with His disciples to prove that He was in form and that He defeated death. Jesus had gone down into the depths of hell and defeated Satan.

Then you have doubting Thomas who was instructed to touch the side of Jesus so he could believe. Some people need their belief restored or healed. They may need to be delivered from doubt and confusion. They need the Thomas experience. Jesus instructed Thomas to touch His side. It was then when Thomas believed that Jesus was and is real and that He rose from the dead. What was the blessing when Thomas touched Jesus, and made the statement that most people in the word remembers, "My Lord and My God". Jesus said, blessed are those who have not seen and yet have believed. My Lord and My God, Your love has touched me and made me to believe. Ask God to touch you today that you may reign in His Kingdom forever and ever.

Sometimes in our lives we think like the woman with the issue of blood who touched Jesus' garment and was made whole by her touch. But the fact of the matter is that it was faith in Him; and more importantly it was His touch that healed her more than her reaching out. The power of healing is in His hand. The power of love is in Him. Blessed be the Name of the Lord.

BECOME ONE IN YOUR MARRIAGE

GENESIS 3:23-24 And Adam said: This is now bone of my bones And flesh of my flesh; She shall be called Woman, Because she was taken out of Man. Therefore a man shall leave his father and mother and be joined to his wife, and they shall become one flesh.

The Bible is very specific about marriages that are made by God. God ordained marriage between a man and woman only, as a union to produce children and as man and wife. God instituted marriage and no one can break it. The other marriage is between God and His church, His saints (Rev 19). These are the only marriages blessed by God Himself in accordance with Gen 3: 23-24 and Mark 10:6-9 God does not want man to drift into the mindset of people described in Romans 1:18-32.

When people fall or step out of true matrimony, they open the gates of hell and demons into their lives. The enemy starts to feed off of the weaknesses and wickedness of people. Then they fall for anything the enemy throws at them. The enemy makes it look good and feel good. He distorts their minds and spirits to make people believe that sin is good. Sin is a trap from the devil. You need to understand that the enemy is the author of lies and confusion. You must get your life on track with Jesus. He wants to destroy your blessed marriage. Keep the vows that you and the priest of the house promised to live by. Love each other with the fullness of love and passion.

Keep your marriage in prayer and before God at all times. He will bless it. You do not have to allow your marriage to become a tragedy and victim of the enemy. Instead walk in the victory daily under His saving grace and power of love. You deserve to be blessed by God. Your loved ones and all of your family deserve to be blessed. Anyone who believes in God knows that there are tricks all day long. And that evil exists to tear you apart. Evil wants to take you over so you will not have a loving family. Those that marry outside of God's authority are opening themselves up for evil to take them over completely. Those who love the Lord are

47

praying that all people come on one accord and be blessed by God's true marriage principles.

Marriage can be complicated to so many people. But in reality it is not complicated. Too many Christian's marriages fail because they stop trusting in God to lead the marriage. God has to be the center of the marriage. God has to be the center of each individual person life to make it work. So then marriage is defined by your relationship with God.

You remember the wedding day. You made a commitment before and on the wedding day with perhaps hundreds of people in attendance or just a few as witnesses. Marriages fail and fall apart because of those who once believed in the power of love from Jesus Christ left the sacredness of their vows. You have to recall that God ordained your marriage. Your marriage is your marriage; it does not belong to anyone else.

Marriage does require attraction, love and affection. We are not to stop showing love and affection, because we love Jesus and must obey Him. He wants you to reveal your love to one another daily. God will restore your marriage. He will strengthen your marriage.

What kind of marriage do you want? Most people want a marriage made in heaven. God wants you to have that kind of marriage as well and enjoy your bride as a gift. Likewise He wants the wife to enjoy her husband. Your marriage can be a marriage made in heaven if you trust God and work at it. Do not allow outside forces, other people or evil spirits to influence your relationship negatively. Go to God for counseling if you need it. Do not get me wrong, God did put other experts to be used as well. Take everything to the Lord and do not hold back. He is your primary and key counselor for all circumstances. Trust Him and He will bless you and maintain your marriage for His appointed duration of your lives together.

THE BEST GIFT EVER!

John 4:9-10 Then the woman of Samaria said to Him, "How is it that You, being a Jew, ask a drink from me, a Samaritan woman?" For Jews have no dealing with Samaritans. Jesus answered and said to her, " If you knew the gift of God, and

who it is who says to you, Give Me a drink , you would have asked Him, and He would have given you living water.

God gave us the ultimate Gift. He gave us His Son Jesus Christ. He is the best gift that can ever been given. He sacrificed His own son for every person on earth and to destroy the work of sin. God is the only true living and loving God. There is no one like Him in all creation. He is the only one who can give such gifts. After the death, burial and resurrection of Jesus, God gave us the Holy Spirit to help us. It was after the ascension of Jesus to heaven when the Holy Spirit would come to help us with our life issues. The Holy Spirit is our gift that God gave us to be there when we need a guide and comfort through life.

God planted His Spirit in man when He breathed the breath of life into Adam's body. Before Adam became a spirit filled man, he was just a man in a dirt suit, made by God only. He was fashioned by God. He was made of God with a clay body. God gave Adam the best gift. He gave Him His Spirit and created Him in His image. So then gifts are one of God's special expressions of blessings in the life of the believer. That is exactly why I stated, if you knew the gift.

One of the things that God wants for His people is to understand that there is no difference between the Jews, Gentiles, and Samaritans. God sent Jesus to wash the sin from all people on earth. In Romans 1:16, the Apostle Paul made a statement that there is neither Jew nor Gentile. He said, "For I am not ashamed of the gospel of Christ, for it is the power of God to salvation for everyone who believes, for the Jew first and also for the Greek." The Apostle Paul, under the anointing of the Holy Spirit wanted everyone to know the Good News. The good news was the news of salvation which had then and now the power to change people's lives. He was not ashamed of the Gospel of Jesus Christ because it has the power to deliver a sin-sick soul from that condition to claiming a place in heaven upon the return of Christ. That is the gift of God for all sick men.

No one was exempted from the salvation that God gave us. No one was too special that they could be turned down. No one is better than another person to receive the blessing of eternal life. If that were so, then Jesus would have had to come as a sacrifice for specific people who could earn their way into the Kingdom of Heaven. The Lord wants us to know that whoever you are under the sun, He can change your life.

At first, the Samaritan woman could not grasp who Jesus was. It took Jesus telling her about herself. He began to tell her that she had five men in her life and the one she was with was not her husband. With conviction and surprise, she believes that He is a prophet.

Much like many other people in this world who believe that someone else is better, she was in total amazement. Jesus told this Samaritan woman that, "If you knew the gift of God and what He could do for you..." It's time to stop searching for the wrong God and the wrong religion. If you get caught up on the wrong God, life will steer you under the devil's influence. That is exactly why Jesus is the gift to people. Recognize Him as Savior and life becomes better. The enemy has no place in your life. Give God the glory!

CHAPTER 3
GOD SEEKERS!

MATTHEW 6:33 But seek first the kingdom of God and His righteousness, and all these things shall be added to you.

When you seek God, it will help to get into the right mind and attitude. God will help to ride you of that high mind, high attitude, high personality that could create problems in your character. God is the one who rocks the pedestal in the life of every person. When God intervenes in your life, you will change directions and become a God-seeker. The God that you will seek is the only true and wise God of Abraham, Isaac, and Jacob. You will seek the God who created heaven and earth by His words. There is no one like Him! Praise His name!

This was a sermon on the mount by Jesus. Jesus was preaching to people that they needed to seek out God as priority over things in this world. We are to seek salvation because it is more precious than all the riches and all the high positions in the world. The word seek means simply to go after something. The Greek word is zeteo which means desire, to investigate, to inquire of something and to search for. God wants us to desire the right things in life and investigate things for the purpose of advancing His Kingdom. His priority is that all of us seek Him and be saved rather than worry about the riches of this world.

In Matthew 6:33, He states "But seek first the kingdom of God and His righteousness, and all these things shall be added to you." Today is your day to make life changes. Ask the Holy Spirit to help you change your old ways to a Godly person who will please God. Make Him your priority in life to seek first the kingdom of God and His righteousness. So many people seek everything else in life such as a new home, cars, the right companion or spouse, fantasy vacations, retirement and so many other things. But the truth of the matter is that God comes first. The Lord knows who is putting Him first in their lives. He will bless you in the overflow. He will touch your life and make you prosper. Stop listening to those that tell you the opposite. Just in case you want to drop a word to them, ask them who they are seeking in life? The inheritance you get from God is eternal and never exhausted. People can bless you; but they bless you differently than God. Continue to concentrate and seek Jesus first and seek Jesus always.

Jesus is the Alpha and Omega, the first and last. That means you have everything you need to survive in life. When you get Jesus, you have eternal life. You live and reign with Jesus eternally. He cannot end but we in the flesh and carnal state will perish. We must be born again to live with Him

At one point in my life, basic training was the most important event for me to achieve. I had made up my mind that I was going to be a soldier and serve the Armed Forces for several years. My focus became clear. I needed to get through those eight agonizing weeks of hell with those crazy Drill Sergeants. If I could make it through all demanding physical training and the draining mental effects, then I knew that I could be called a United States Armed Forces "soldier" When you know that you are a real soldier, and then you know that everything that you sought after was rewarding in life. I can rest now knowing that those years and that training was not done in vain

I liken my military career to seeking first the Lord's Kingdom and His righteousness. I need the help of the Holy Spirit in God's Army. Nothing can be sought after and achieved kingdom-wise if you do not have the Holy Spirit working in you. As a Christian today, sometimes I believe that I need to revisit God's Basic training camp. I need a special tune up. I need the Lord to take hold of me and make me over. When He makes me over, I will be able to see the reality of seeking Him first. It is more than what we think. What is clear to me now is that I must put God first, no matter what.

There are various kinds of people in the world. Some enjoy the outdoor game of hunting. When you hunt, you are searching for the kill of the game. God wants that kind of attitude in His children. Some hunters score big points for big game. This is the kind of game that one can prepare for a meal. Some is transformed into trophies. The same happens when you play football and basketball. The best players are highlighted and given huge contracts.

GET THAT WEIGHT OFF OF ME!

HEBREW 12:1 Therefore, since we are surrounded by such a huge crowd of witnesses to the life of faith, let us strip off every weight that slows us down, especially the sin that so easily trips us up. And let us run with endurance the race God has set before us.

Today you are a weight loser. You specialize in losing weight. You did what you had to do to drop those excessive pounds and you feel good now. Health is good for you. Too much weight will clog your arteries. Too much weight will give you back pain and stress. Too much weight will hinder your faith walk. Too much weight will cause you to have a heart attack, depression, and illnesses of all kinds. If I were to caution you today, I would say go on a diet if you have too much weight.

Seriously do a fast to break the bondage of overeating. I met several people that let their body go. They allowed too much weight to come on and became sick. Some allowed their appearance to get out of control. Don't allow the enemy to give you excessive excuses and excessive weight in an effort to kill you. In the Christian world we need to take off weight so that we can witness to people.

Sin is what causes it all. Sin slows people down. Take an inventory of what slows you down as though it was a heavy weight in the flesh and in the spirit. You may find that one weight is that you do not have a relationship with Jesus Christ.

Today, turn to Jesus and get a positive and strong attitude. Get that joy and confidence back. Start with an unshakable attitude. When you get Jesus in your life that is when your attitude changes for the good. It's Holy and with power, then God will use you. Think about having a powerful and positive Godly attitude.

You can run the race set before you with a positive attitude. Those things that you use to weigh you down must fall off. Put off those weights and put on God.

You can be weighed down with all kinds of sins on you that are harmful such as adultery and lust. A family is broken as a result of hatred, jealousy, envy, strife or even an evil spirit and negative attitude.

In order to live the good life, you need to be healthy and full of strength. Put off the weight and put on God. Put on God by surrendering your will to Him. Put on God by serving and becoming a dedicated witness. This is healthy for you and helps fulfill your purpose in life.

Weights are unhealthy. Being over weight is unhealthy. Our Father did not create us to be unhealthy. Set new goals in your life today to exercise your faith, body, mind and spirit. Women exercise your 'spirit woman' as a mother training up her children and nurturing them. If we want to be healthy in our bodies we must eat the proper food groups. You will be happier and feel better. You will also live longer. If we want to be healthy in spirit, we need to fast and study the word of God. That is what breaks demonic strongholds and bondages.

Get ready, because you are about to run the race of your life. Tell the enemy to go back to hell and stay there. Tell him,"You have no business trying to interrupt my life in Jesus name. I am a runner for Jesus. Get out of the way because you will get run over in Jesus name. I rebuke all demons in my way, all demons in my family and friend's way in Jesus name."

You need to maintain a proper diet because it is essential for your health. Take a look at the proper breads, fish, dairy products, fruits and vegetables. Take the necessary portions each day to maintain a healthy diet. You already know how to discipline yourself. If you do not know how to start a proper diet, seek God and a nutritionist to develop a plan for your life. Then stick with that plan. Apply it in the spirit as well.

When you start your diet, just think of it as going on a diet for the Lord. You can also go on a fast as well. The two key things about both of them are that they result in a breakthrough and a balanced life. As time goes by, you will see that God is working in your life. You will live a better life. You can do it. Do not let yourself go down for anybody! Live for God! Live for you! Live for your family! Don't you give up on God! Your health means a lot to the Lord. He gave you this earthen vessel to take care of it. You are not to worship it, but to live a good life. I was thinking of the proper diet spoken earlier. When you go on a diet, imagine how you study the word of God. Well use that method of training your body. At the same time, when you are fasting and praying, you will also get a breakthrough if you are vigorously doing it. Fasting gets your spiritual breakthrough.

HIS HANDS ARE FULL OF POWER

John 20:19-21 Then, the same day at evening, being the first day of the week, when the doors were shut where the disciples were assembled, for fear of the Jews, Jesus came and stood in the midst, and said to them, "Peace be with you." When He had said this, He showed them His hands and His side. Then the disciples were glad when they saw the Lord. So Jesus said to them again, "Peace to you! As the Father has sent Me, I also send you."

His hands have power to send you out to bless somebody! What is in your hands? We are always putting something inside our hands like a pen, pencil, eating utensil, or documents.   Many of us have craftsman's hands. Jesus had craftsman hands; as He was a carpenter. Nevertheless when He went to Calvary those same hands, men put huge nails in, as they crucified Him to a cross. Who would have thought that men could be so cruel and evil to someone so perfect and spotless? But He was sent to be a spotless Lamb and sacrifice for a world of sinners. Yes, you guessed it even the ones who crucified Him. Jesus said, Father forgive them for they know not what they do. Are the tears rolling down your face, yet? Who would have ever guessed or known that the same hands that nails went into are the same hands that would comfort a broken sinner like me? He is at the right hand of the Father in Heaven and holds the world in the palm of His hands. He is the son of the living God.   He is always revealing miracles and demonstrating His love again and again. Thank God that He is always taking care of us. I am reminded when Jesus showed us the picture of forgiveness with a woman caught in adultery. He stooped down and wrote something in the ground with his finger. No one is sure what He wrote, some think it was the Ten Commandments and some think it was the sin of the Pharisees and scribes, and some believe he wrote a message to the Pharisees. Nevertheless, those accusers could not trap him and they left his presence. Jesus told her to go and sin no more. Jesus never pointed at her. He simply forgave her. The Law is not more powerful than the love of Christ. Nothing is more powerful than the Lord's power to forgive and love His children.

As I was playing with my granddaughter, I realized how tiny and unique she is. She was acting all grown up. I placed her hand in my hand and really just looked back again to see how tiny her hands really were. I was playing the little game, Itsy Bitsy Spider with her and what got me is when she just stared at my hand. I kept showing her my fingers and placing her hand in my hand. Something about that moment just blessed me and struck me in complete awe and amazement of God's gentleness and loving kindness.

I thought about the hand of God. God's hand touches us and heals us. God's hands have all power. The Father's hands never have to really touch anything because He is God. However we can reach out and receive the hand of God. Our Father's hand covers us every time we are in need and every day that we breathe. Every time we need Him to lift us up from falling into the pits, He reaches out His hand of unfailing love and mercy. Every time we stumble into the enemy's camp, He reaches out His hand to place us on the right path of life. Every time we drift back into the mindset of sinful living, He reaches out His hand to find and rescue us. He is the one that left the ninety-nine to show His love in the life of that one who was lost. The writer says, "Do not remove your hand from me. Every time we call on Him in marriage situations, He knows exactly where to place His hand. It's in his hands; a touch of power transcends imagination. If His hands touch us, we are healed. If His hands touch us, we are restored. Allow Jesus to touch you today! Allow Him to touch your life that He may put you on the path of righteousness.

When Thomas doubted about the resurrection, it was Jesus who told him to put his hand in His side and in the nail prints in His hand. The purpose was so that Thomas would believe in Jesus' resurrection. Then Jesus said that those who have not seen shall surely be blessed. Thomas needed to touch Him to see if He is real.

Today is your day. If you want to find out if Jesus can touch you with His loving hands, ask Him to come into your life. Receive salvation for it is eternal and you will reign in His Kingdom Forever. His hand will keep you in perfect peace on earth. His hand will bless you in ways you cannot imagine.

RECOVER IN JESUS NAME!

2 Corinthians 12:9 And He said to me, "My grace is sufficient for you, for My strength is made perfect in weakness." Therefore most gladly I will rather boast in my infirmities, that the power of Christ may rest upon me.

While riding down the back roads conducting military missions, all of sudden, there was a loud explosion that hit our vehicle and flipped it, leaving casualties and wounded personnel. In many cases, we would have just finished a card game or dominoes or even a phone call with a special woman. Then hell breaks loose on the camp with mortar rounds landing everywhere. We never thought Baghdad would change our lives that much. If you served in the military and are back home now, life may seem devastating to you.

Before we go any further, please understand that whatever you went through, Jesus Christ is your answer now. He can help you recover from all of that pain, suffering and scars. Listen fellow soldier; Jesus Christ can help you recover no matter what you have experienced. His grace is sufficient. It is not deserved, however, it is sufficient. This means He gives you strength and can remove the scars of combat. If anyone tells you that He cannot, it is not the truth. You have to trust in Jesus to help you the rest of your life. Go to church this Sunday and start praying and worshipping Him!

All of those times we had our game face on observing every obstacle, scoping out every potential Improvised Explosive Device (IED); when the enemy was still out there hiding and waiting for his moment to hit another vehicle to cause casualties. We still needed to know God for ourselves. Everybody knows now that an easy day can turn into your worst nightmare, when you least expect it. One couldn't help but to wonder whether or not God truly loved you while all of those things were happening. When you step on battle ground in war, you need to understand that it is ugly and there is no way around ugliness in war. When we engaged in direct enemy fire, there were explosions everywhere. Listen my friend and fellow soldiers, Jesus Christ can heal you. Read about the Centurion soldier. When Jesus had entered Capernaum; a centurion came to him, asking for help. "Lord," he said, "my servant lies at home paralyzed, suffering terribly." Jesus said to him, "Shall I come and heal him?" The centurion replied, "Lord, I do not deserve to have you come under my roof. But just say the word, and my servant will be healed. For myself I am a man under authority, with soldiers under me. I tell this one, 'Go,' and he goes; and that one, 'Come,' and he comes. I say to my servant, 'Do this,' and he does it." When Jesus heard this, He was amazed and said to those following him, "Truly I tell you, I have not found anyone in Israel with such great faith. I say to you that many will come from the east and the west, and will take their places at the feast with Abraham, Isaac and Jacob in the kingdom of heaven. But the subjects of the kingdom will be thrown outside, into the darkness, where there will be weeping and gnashing of teeth (Matthew 8:5-13)." Then Jesus said to the centurion, "Go! Let it be done just as you believed it would." And his servant was healed at that moment. Jesus has the healing power for all soldiers. His grace is even in his healing by faith.

He always reminds us of his grace. The scripture above always comes to mind that His grace is sufficient even in my darkest hours in the war zone. Some days even when things seem calm, you are still saying get me out of this hell hole of disaster and killings. It is already enough to be wondering about if I am going to heaven or hell. It is another thing to think that I am fighting because someone else made a decision to send me. It is the grace of God that kept me through all the battles and explosions. It is important that all soldiers recover under grace. You can go to Jesus, anytime. He will heal a broken spirit and wounded soldier like you and I.

BLESSED IN AND OUT OF THE PIT

GEN 37:23 So when Joseph came to his brothers, they stripped him of his robe, the richly oriented robe he was wearing. And they took him and threw him into the cistern. Now the cistern was empty; there was no water in it. So when the Midianites merchants came by, his brothers pulled Joseph up out of the cistern and sold him for twenty shekels of silver to the Ishmaelite, who took him to Egypt.

Joseph was stripped by his brothers and thrown into a pit. His brothers and His entire family did not understand the anointing on his life in the beginning of the messages. They did not have the vision, or the dreams he had. Joseph's brothers thought that they had broken his spirit. Instead they just pushed him into the favor of God. They stripped him down for the purpose of getting rid of their father's favorite son. They did not know that by stripping him of the coat of many colors, they set him up for God's favor and blessings. There is no way to stop the blessings that God has in store for you and me. Certainly, Joseph's blessings were not going to be stopped. When the Lord sets something in motion, it will not be stopped by anyone or anything.

Joseph's coat was representation of royalty. His father gave it to him because he favored him. Joseph coat is viewed as a rainbow for the covenant God made with Noah, no more floods. Some see the coat as a representation of a priest. His father saw it as a gift and a blessing for his son. We need to know that God has made all of us royal priests in the Army of the Lord. We need to know that when we have family situations, God does not turn His back on us. There are blessings on the way. The robe was a blessing and that is exactly why the enemy wanted to twist things in the family, causing jealousy. It is clear that when Jesus rose from the dead, He wore a priestly robe.

Jealousy can cause all kinds of trouble. But when trouble comes our way, God makes everything alright. He walks with us and protects us. The Pharisees were jealous of Jesus because He went about healing, making miracles happen, and teaching disciples. Jesus was punished because of the jealousy of the Pharisees and His own people. Joseph was punished by his blood brothers. No matter how much you feel like somebody has broken you like a slave, keep your head up and look to the hills where you help comes from. Jesus always looked to the Father when things got rough. He prayed in the Garden of Gethsemane. Joseph kept the faith in knowing who his God was during the tough times..

You have an advocate who will defeat the enemy. He will set you up for blessings too innumerable to count. He is ready to help you when someone sells you out. God is always on your side. You can be just like Joseph and be positioned according to God's favor and will for your life. Do not give up even if you feel like you have be placed in a pit, left for dead, then sold like a piece of meat. You need to ask God, our heavenly Father to pull you out of the pit. God is on your side and He has multiple blessings for you. He will pull you out of the pit and place you in a palace. Your success depends on God. Your recovery depends on God. You need to know that God strips all of us.

BE ON FIRE FOR GOD!

REV 3:15-16 I know your works, that you are neither cold nor hot, I could wish you were cold or hot. So then, because you are lukewarm, and neither cold nor hot, I will vomit you out of My mouth.

God sees everything and hears everything from the Throne Room of Heaven. He knows the ability of the church. He knows the ability of those who proclaim His name. He knows who has backslidden and fallen from the faith. He knows what caused it and who caused it and the situation behind it. God is no respecter of persons. No one can hide. No one can get away with anything. He is omnipresent and omniscient. He is looking for a church without spot or wrinkle. God knows the heart of man. God knows the heart of the Church.

The Lord wants men to have a heart that is on fire for Him. He said, be either cold or hot. The point is to go all the way for Him. He wants men to have a servant's hearts that will continue in obedience. He wants men to follow in His will for their lives and the ministry of the Gospel.

Do you remember the first time you felt the change and the conversion? You were on fire for the Lord. God is saying do not leave your first love. He was there when you first fell in love with Him. You read the word and were on fire for the Lord. Do not let somebody or something steal your joy and force you to walk away from the anointing on your life. The enemy is deceitful and divisive enough to make you think otherwise. He comes to steal, kill and to destroy your dreams, hopes, joy, peace, service for the Lord and your life. You do not have to stand by and let the enemy snatch it all away. Listen to the voice of the Lord.

Noah did not allow it; he was on fire for the Lord. He built an ark and saved the world from total devastation. He saved his family and helped restore creation. Abraham was on fire. He moved when God told Him to move. He move by faith to the place God told him to go. He became the Father of many nations. God has something in store for you. You are a child of the Most High, so start walking in the anointing placed in your life.

You might lose some friends. But God is on your side. Besides, no one can get you into heaven, but God. 2 Timothy 1:6 also encourages the believer to be on fire for God. He states, in 2 Timothy 1:6 wherefore I put thee in remembrance of that thou stir up the gift of God, which is in thee by the putting on of my hands. It is also interpreted as to fan the flames. When you fan the flames, the fire increases with power to preach, witness and serve God. This means the fire does not go out! The gift he refers to is the Holy Spirit who has power that exceeds fire, however that can help you and I make a difference in somebody's life. In other words, fire leaves an effect. The Christian who walks with the gift of God will be on fire, leaving a lasting effect on other people's lives as a witness in God's Kingdom. Tell someone about Jesus Christ. Ask God to stir up the gift in you in your preaching, if you are a minister, Be on fire for the Lord today and win a soul to God's Kingdom. You can do it, be encouraged saints.

VICTORY OVER ALL ENEMIES!

1 JOHN 5:4-5 For whatever is born of God overcomes the world. And this is the victory that has overcome the world-our faith. Who is he who overcomes the world, but he who believes that Jesus is the son of God.

Faith is being born of God. Faith is the power of God reflecting in your life. When you are born of God, you have the victory. You will upset the devil and his demons. No one can walk victorious without Jesus in their heart. You must have faith to be an overcomer of the world and its system. The world is tricky because it is attractive to so many people. It has so much that looks well and entices a person to live a life without Christ. It is vitally important that you make Jesus the head of your life, today. Do not wait any longer. It is like suicide without Him. He will bless you more than you know. You get yourself up and you make it happen with the Lord. You tell Jesus that you want to make a date, time and place for the two of you to meet. You talk to the Lord for yourself. When you get Christ Jesus in your life, you can tell any and everybody that no one can snatch victory away from you. . Make a change and walk in victory.

Don't misunderstand the blessings that God gives us in this world. Do not get caught up with all the things that are not of God. As a soldier in the Army, I remember telling about 64,000 soldiers or more about what the Bible says is victory in the Lord. I was absolutely shocked when I was able to tell some of the highest ranking officers and enlisted men that nothing is better than having victory in the Lord. You see victory comes directly from Him. Our strength, knowledge, technical skills, strategies, decision making, creativity, and abilities had to come from the One who holds and gives intellect to man.

It must be faith in God that drives senior leadership and subordinate leaders and the soldiers to secure victory in war and battle. Faith must be the cornerstone. It must be the absolute ingredient in the heart of man that gets him to victory.

Victory is not optional when it comes to saints of the Lord. We have it in Christ, and it will not be changed because He promised it. Victory relies on faith. You must have faith. It can be the faith of a mustard seed. It can be the faith of a person newly converted, as long as that faith is true Godly faith. The faith you have whether you are in Iraq, Afghanistan, Africa, Asia, Korea, Kuwait or even the United States is the faith needed to believe in Jesus and accept Him in your heart as Lord and Savior. Then, you will walk in a continuous life of victory in the Lord.

You can start over from where you are now. You are never too low. Read Psalms 139. God said if you make your bed in hell, He is there. He will not leave you. Certainly, if you have fallen from the faith, God is there to pick you up again. Let the Lord carry you. You just ask the Holy Spirit to ignite your heart that it will be on fire again for the service of the Lord. The Bible says to pick up your cross and carry it. When you are on fire, God will use you to glorify Him.

It is time to pick up your sword again. Pick up your Bible and read it again. The enemy has worked hard trying to destroy you. Some of your companions worked hard to keep you down. If they are encouraging you, then fine; but if not you might have to break away. Do not let anyone tamper with your soul's salvation. Be strong in the Lord and in the power of His might. Stay focused and God will see you through.

Preach the word and be instant in season and out of season. Tell of God's plan of salvation. Be a witness on fire and tell everyone that God loves them more than anybody could even imagine. Tell them that God listens to a repentant heart. Tell them that God has a plan for them and for you. Remember to keep the faith and let the love of God be shed abroad in your heart by the power of the Holy Spirit. Praise His righteous name forever.

PRAYER IN YOUR FASTING HOURS

Matthew 4:1-12 Then Jesus was led up by the Spirit into the

wilderness to be tempted by the devil. And when He had fasted forty days and forty nights, afterward He was hungry. [3] Now when the tempter came to Him, he said, "If You are the Son of God, command that these stones become bread." "But He answered and said, "It is written, *'Man shall not live by bread alone, but by every word that proceeds from the mouth of God.'* Then the devil took Him up into the holy city, set Him on the pinnacle of the temple, and said to Him, "If You are the Son of God, throw Yourself down. For it is written:

> **' *He shall give His angels charge over you,'* and,**
> **' *In their hands they shall bear you up,***
> ***Lest you dash your foot against a stone."***

Jesus said to him, "It is written again, *'You shall not tempt the LORD your God.'* Again, the devil took Him up on an exceedingly high mountain, and showed Him all the kingdoms of the world and their glory. And he said to Him, "All these things I will give You if You will fall down and worship me." Then Jesus said to him, "Away with you, Satan! For it is written, *'You shall worship the LORD your God, and Him only you shall serve."* Then the devil left Him, and behold, angels came and ministered to Him. Now when Jesus heard that John had been put in prison, He departed to Galilee.

Jesus began His Galilean ministry after He fasted for forty days. When you fast and pray, you may have a wilderness experience that will change the course of your life. Jesus had an experience that was set by the Father in heaven.

It appears that one of the most effective ways to begin your ministry is by fasting and praying. This allows you to seek the Lord and get closer to Him. Fasting opens up channels of communication between you and God. You get the connection properly when you leave flesh out of the matter at hand. God loves it when we put our plates aside for a while. He wants us to fast privately and not publically announce it. It is personal between you and God alone. God wants us to have breakthroughs. Jesus illustrated exactly what we need to do. We fast and use the word of God against the enemy, who chases us daily. We fast to get the mission done. We fast out of devotion to Christ Jesus to let go of things that entangle us and bind us. We fast and pray because we are committed to live a life in Christ Jesus.

Today, ask yourself what is it that I need to fast from that has a necessary hold on me? If you need it each day and can't do without it (except for water), then it may have a hold on you. When you fast, get ready for some attacks because you operate in the spirit, even more. Also remember that God is on your side whenever you are going through. It is important that you seek God before fasting. Ask the Lord to help you make the right choice. When you fast, you do not have to boast about it and tell everyone. It is between you and God. However, you can share with your spouse. If the community churches are fasting together, it is necessary to keep each other in prayer. Seek your breakthrough in Christ Jesus.

OVERCOME YOUR PARALYZED CONDITION

Matthew 9:1-8 So He got into a boat, crossed over, and came to His own city. Then behold, they brought to Him a paralytic lying on a bed. When Jesus saw their faith, He said to the paralytic, "Son, be of good cheer; your sins are forgiven you." And at once some of the scribes said within themselves, "This Man blasphemes!" But Jesus, knowing their thoughts, said, "Why do you think evil in your hearts? For which is easier, to say, '*Your* sins are forgiven you,' or to say, 'Arise and walk'? But that you may know that the Son of Man has power on earth to forgive sins"—then He said to the paralytic, "Arise, take up your bed, and go to your house." And he arose and departed to his house. Now when the multitudes saw *it,* they marveled[l] and glorified God, who had given such power to men.

This day is your day to get out of the paralyzed conditions of life. Your sins are already forgiven you. It was forgiven by the power of Jesus Christ. He took the sting out of death, overcame the grave and all principalities. It may seem impossible, but it is not.

Nothing is impossible for the Lord. Jesus said on the cross, "It is finished!" It may seem as though no one cares or will help you, but that is not the truth. God alone is able to do the impossible for you. Today is your day to arise and walk. You have the power if you believe in Jesus Christ, who rose from the dead.

You probably encountered a person in a wheel chair or crippled for some reason. There are some things we do not have the power to do in our own strength. But the God of second chances, the God of healing power and miracles can change things in an instant.

There are many people who feel like their hurt will never go away as if it was eternal. But inside their heart, is a crippled mentality which is even worse than a physical one. That religious mentality keeps them from accepting Jesus as Lord of their life.

I once watched a man on television preaching the gospel with a scarred face. His legs were severed in a car accident. So now he lives his life without legs. But he does not go around sad and acting like he has no hope. Instead, he gives all that he has to service for Christ. He inspired me to a new level of thinking.

Believers all over the world should see this man who has the tenacity to walk in faith and be healed in mind, soul, and spirit. He believes that Jesus is his Lord and there is no other like Him. This is your time for healing so get it! Keep the faith and walk in it. Believe that God can remove any crippling situation in your life. Stop allowing your past sins to create barriers and brokenness in your life. Instead listen to what Jesus said, "Arise and walk. Your sins have been forgiven."

BE FRUITFUL

GALATIONS 5:21-26 But the fruit of the Spirit is love, joy, peace, longsuffering, kindness, goodness, faithfulness, gentleness, self-control. Against such there is no law. And those who are Christ's have crucified the flesh with its passions and desires. If we live in the Spirit, let us also walk in the Spirit. Let us not become conceited, provoking one another, envying one another.

You need patience in just about everything you do. More importantly, you have to have patience to walk in faith in God. If you are confident in God, you do not have to give into anything in this world. The Fruit of the Spirit will cause you to prosper in life.

The scripture reads, but the fruit of the Spirit is love, joy, peace, longsuffering, kindness, goodness, faithfulness, gentleness, and self-control. What a combination to live with. When you express a fruitful lifestyle to God, He knows. He wants us to live with other people around us so that they will have the power of Jesus' love and touch. These fruit are a must if you want to be successful. Patience wins no matter what the obstacle or barrier may be. If you are sketching on a canvas, it will require patience.

PASSOVER

EXODUS 12:13-17 Now the blood shall be a sign for you on the houses where you are. And when I see the blood, I will pass over you; and the plague shall not be on you to destroy you when I strike the land of Egypt. 'So this day shall be to you a memorial; and you shall keep it as a feast to the LORD throughout your generations. You shall keep it as a feast by an everlasting ordinance.

Seven days, you shall eat unleavened bread. On the first day, you shall remove leaven from your houses. For whoever eats leavened bread from the first day until the seventh day, that person shall be cut off from Israel. On the first day, there shall be a holy convocation, and on the seventh day there shall be a holy convocation for you. No manner of work shall be done on them; but that which everyone must eat—that only may be prepared by you. So you shall observe the Feast of Unleavened Bread, for on this same day I will have brought your armies out of the land of Egypt. Therefore you shall observe this day throughout your generations as an everlasting ordinance. Our Lord Jesus is the Lamb of God made the sacrifice. His blood covers us.

The Exodus is one of the most important events in Jewish history when comes to God's people. The Exodus is when God freed His people from the slavery and bondage of Egyptian task masters. Before God had set the Israelites free from Egypt, He had commanded them to eat the Passover meal. Jesus in Mark 16 and John 19 and 1 Corinthians 11 is our sacrifice and risen Savior in whom we partake in communion of the Lord. His body is broken for me. His blood washed me whiter than snow. His blood is the redeeming power that took away sin.

This time was like no other. God sent not rain or a storm to take care of sin in this land. During this particular time, God had had enough of this wickedness with Pharaoh. God is not someone who plays with others. God is serious and loving. He is just and merciful. This night a death angel would be pouring out death, door to door. People are in expectation and anticipation of God outpouring of blessings. In this particular time, they weren't blessings.

Our children need a down pour today to keep them from falling prey to sin. Too many teenagers are living to impress their peers. Peer pressure is one of the leading causes of children stumbling. You have the ability to do anything. Our children have to stop being idle. It is time to live out dreams. No one can stop you from living your dream. The enemy wants to carry out his version of this scripture and wipe you out. The only sure way of not being wiped out is to accept Jesus as Lord and Savior.

It is time for fathers to be the priests in the house. And mothers need to be the true help meet start marking your homes. It is time to start identifying and equipping young people who have talent to work hard and be successful.

AUTHORITY AND POWER FROM HEAVEN

LUKE 10:18-22 And He said to them, "I saw Satan fall like lightning from heaven. Behold, I give you the authority to trample on serpents and scorpions, and over all the power of the enemy, and nothing shall by any means hurt you. Nevertheless do not rejoice in this, that the spirits are subject to you, but rather rejoice because your names are written in heaven." In that hour Jesus rejoiced in the Spirit and said, "I thank You, Father, Lord of heaven and earth, that You have hidden these things from *the* wise and prudent and revealed

them to babes. Even so, Father, for so it seemed good in Your sight. All things have been delivered to Me by My Father, and no one knows who the Son is except the Father, and who the Father is except the Son, and *the one* to whom the Son wills to reveal *Him.*"

God used His power and authority to send Lucifer now Satan from Heaven to hell. He kicked him out. Now he is an enemy of the household of God. He still has all authority and power. Imagine it! Just imagine God could have used a simple thought to kick Lucifer out of heaven faster than striking. He did not even have to use his pinky finger. God is bad to bone! He is Glorious and mighty! Give Him Praise! Take a moment and give him praise. Remove your pride and praise Him. The same God has already predestined Satan to the Lake of Fire. He will handle him according to His word. It's a done deal.

God is so powerful that everything must bow before Him. And everything must worship Him in the beauty of His Holiness. No one is exempt from bowing down (Philippians 2). Noah found grace for several reasons. It's important for us to know, so we can be obedient like Noah was in building the ark. Noah was cheered on by God. He did not wait for another cheering section. He knew that God would inspire Him because it was God who spoke to him. Noah found grace because he loved the Lord. Noah found grace because of His obedience to do what God said, no matter what people around him were saying.

Noah found grace because he listened and heard what God had to say. Noah found grace because it was in God's plan

Lightning comes down fast. It will hit whatever is in the path. This is probably the only time in my life when I am happy to hear about lightening. This lightening is for the sake of getting rid of something. What is so unique about this word is that God said, I give you authority to trample on serpents and scorpions. God also gives us power to call down the rain in our lives when we have a dry spell. God is able to make His servants rejoice in the time of evil on the battlefield.

BE A MAN OF GOD

Most of us heard so many people say, things such as, "I need a man who is God centered to lead me". Likewise men say, they need a woman that is fixed on God and submissive; not a woman who interferes and allows people outside to enter the relationship to break it up. Most people believe they can trust someone that will display more integrity and faith. This kind of person follows God in his or her daily living. They both want their needs fulfilled.

I want a woman who can be there for me. I want a woman who I don't have to put chains on to keep her from cheating in the streets. I need a woman I can pray over, who appreciates me as a man, protector and provider. When you are a man of God, you need a woman you can trust. She does not sit in the night clubs, waiting on man to make her feel pretty or fill her voids. You need a woman to trust and who looks to God for help. Women want the same thing. A woman
wants a man who will get God in his life and exercise the authority by faith and speak blessings in the house over her and her children.

The husband is the priest in your house. God is the head Priest in your life. Everyone in the house falls under His complete authority. Everyone in the house must know that God ordained husbands to bless the house. God made the order and it is not changing. You just have to live by His order and know it and love it. He orders our footsteps. He orders the marriage because He alone ordained marriage. He orders everyone in the house. He ordained the seed to be birth. He knew which child in the house would be the way they are at this very moment. God knows exactly what each person is in need of for their lives. God, our Lord knows if you honor your father and mother as Ephesians 6 states. It is a good thing to know that the power of God is in your house. So God has His own strategy for your house.

He placed the man as the head of the house because that is simply His order. He desires to keep order in your house. The moment the order is broken, those that assist in breaking the order, have to deal with God. It is God's will for your house to walk in blessings. If you step out of order, the enemy wants to come right in and disrupt.

In the Bible, Job had a visitation. His entire family was wiped out except his wife. All the children were killed by the enemy's attack. But because Job continued to trust and walk in the faith of God, he was blessed with more abundance he ever had. I say this to tell children to obey your father so that it will be pleasing in the sight of God.

In Luke 15, the Prodigal Son did not recognize the extent of the blessing on his father's life and in house. The Prodigal Son left home thinking with arrogance that he could make it on his own and He did not need the blessing and inheritance of his father. But to his surprise, life became complicated and challenging to the utmost, beyond his ability to maintain himself. When you find yourself in a condition that forces you to go to the pig pen and slop around with the swine, you need to get a new attitude and return to God. Jesus is calling now. You do not have to wait until times get difficult, He deserves the praise now. What you see in the story of the Prodigal Son is that the father never lost the ability to shower the blessing of love. He threw a celebration for his son's arrival back home.

There are people today who need to come back home to the Father. He is the priest of the house. He answers to the Most High God. He sets the condition for you to prosper as long as you remain obedient. I tell you that The Father in heaven will never let you down. He will not turn you away. He will never leave you. He specializes in love grace, mercy, salvation, deliverance, blessings and getting all the glory.

If you have a lost son or daughter, do not give in. Do not allow the enemy to take authority; you take it. Do not give up. God is working on them. God is speaking to them at this very moment. Give them a call and ask them what is God saying? Tell them what God is saying to you, as well. Make it a family revival. Open the word at the right time and tell them what scripture the Lord has shared with you. Then pray together. That will make the enemy flee and get mad about his defeat. Your victory is in the Lord Jesus Christ. Jesus, our high Priest is the Lord of Lord and King of Kings. Come back home to the Priest and worship the Father in Heaven with all your heart.

NO LONGER PARALYZED!

Mark 2:4 And when they could not come near Him because of the crowd, they uncovered the roof where He was, so when they had broken through, they let down the bed on which the Paralytic was lying.

Some places allow you to use the front entry. But sometimes the crowd can force you to take a different route. That is what happened with this man who had a paralytic condition. When you need healing, you need to come up with a strategy, positive attitude and a prayer life in Christ. You need to break through some things in life. Do not let the crowd stop you. Let the Lord know your desire. He wants you to use your mind and allow the blessing to be poured out. You have much potential in your imagination; just uncover it for God's purpose. You have an imagination that can cause you to make millions. Ask God to keep you from being paralyzed and restore you. The Greek word for paralyze is paralutikos which means afflicted with paralysis. It also means to disable on one side. Someone could easily be afflicted in their body with a spine injury due to a car wreck or a back injury due to a fall.

In this story, the paralyzed man needed healing. What was so powerful about these men, they were not allowing anything to get in their way. They had already made up their minds that there is a way to get healing. They used their imagination to get to the roof of the building where Jesus was inside. They let the man down to Jesus. These men must be considered God-sent!

We live in a society that have many people who have need of healing. Many lives have been paralyzed by the enemy. They also remain paralyzed because men and their families have not accepted Jesus as Lord and Savior. Today is your day to use your imagination and uncover your heart to let Jesus inside. He will keep you eternally in His hand. If you are around crowds, leave the crowd and go and get saved by Jesus Christ, the Son of the living God. You will never have to be paralyzed again because your spirit belongs to God and no one else.

When I played football, I ran hard and strong over the defenders and had the potential like so many others to play professional football. But something happened to me, in football practice on a rainy and muddy day. I was tackled by, at least, five defenders, who piled on me. They did not realize that my legs had twisted. I left that day with a hip pointer. I had to sit out of the games for a while until I healed properly. In my mind, I lost a little confidence and a little spark because I felt paralyzed. There was no need for me to feel that way. I just told myself that and I want to tell you that you never have feel that way.

Today, if you feel like the enemy has paralyzed you from head to toe and even broken your hip to keep you from running for the Lord, call on the name of Jesus for healing. Call on Him to help you to run for His purpose. Call His Holy and Righteous name. He will be there to lift you up from being paralyzed. God wants you healed from being from paralyzed. Walk in wholeness and healing. You are not a paralyzed man. You are a transformed man in Christ Jesus.

INCREASE

1 CORINTHIANS 3:5-7 Who then is Paul, and who is Apollos, but ministers through Whom you believe as the Lord gave to each one? I planted, Apollos watered, but God gave the increase. So then neither he who plants is anything, nor he who waters, but God who gives the increase.

God gives the increase in every way that He desires. God gave the millionaire actor the ability to use his talents in Hollywood. Because of his ability to act, he increases his income to millions of dollars. But no one can receive an increase unless God gives it. All increases in your assets come from God. All blessings of planting and watering come from God. God is clearly showing all people that all increase comes from Him. We need to understand that God ministers and sends ministers even for increase in your life. Anyway God wants to increase in my life, so be it. When we take our eyes off the prize, then we begin to sink and drown in our own spiritual abilities. Neither Paul nor Apollos gain the credit for service for the Lord. Everything we do must be to glorify His righteous name.

In their preaching, it had to be the Lord who blesses with the power of conversion and conviction. It has to be the power of the Holy Spirit who reveals carnality and those who are in need of being spirit-filled.

The Apostle Paul was tasked with giving the word even to those who were babes in Christ and carnal in mind. 1 Corinthians 3:2 states, I fed you with milk and not with solid food, for until now you were not able to receive it, and even now you are still not able. But in Christ, men of God don't give up. Men might be able to identify weaknesses and what the enemy meant for bad. But God always steps in for good!. You see, it does not depend on these two men for your salvation. But it is dependent upon God, the one who gives the increase.

Churches are not successful because they have great preachers. Churches are successful because The Holy Spirit shows up and does the work that God requires for His glory. Worship is not happening unless the Holy Spirit leads the congregation. Praise from the heart is not going forth unless the Holy Spirit ushers it through the sanctuary and the people. God gives the increase, only He can sanctify. God gives the increase because only He can justify. God gives the increase because He owns the cattle on a thousand hills. God gives the increase because He is the creator of all things. He knows just what to do with whom He chooses. God gives the increase in any way He sees fit. If He wants 100 or 1000 new members in one Church on one set day, He can do it. If He wants 10,000 or 20,000 new members, He can do it. God builds the church, not man. God grows the church and sustain its blessings. The scripture is clear in Psalms 127:1, Except the Lord build a house, they labor in vain that build it; except the Lord keep the city, the watchman waketh but in vain. He has His hand on the pulse of all service and servants. He know what will prosper to give Him glory.

When I was a young boy, I used to think that the man in the pulpit was God's man and he made it happen. It took me to learn of His word and become a minister in His grace to learn of Him and serve Him according to His will.

Today, allow the Holy Spirit to minister to you. Know that He will enter the heart of man and reveal His love to you right now. He will help you to grow in the faith regardless of what happened in the past. Jesus Christ loves you and always shines His tender mercies and grace on your life. Blessings in His Holy Name.

KNOW GOD FOR YOURSELF

Philippians 3:10 that I may know Him and the power of His resurrection, and the fellowship of His sufferings, being conformed to His death.

When you get intimate with God and stay in His word, He will commune with you and your fellowship will become habitual. Your relationship will be stronger than ever before. You will begin to delight yourself in the Lord. You will know Him and experience a glimpse of His resurrection. You will experience even more than you can imagine. An experience with the Lord is more than enough. It is a life of fulfillment. You will never want anything outside of His perfect will and touch for your life. Know Him for yourself. Scripture says, "To know Him and the power of His resurrection" Imagine knowing Him!
Your heart changes when you know Him. More blessings come when you know Him. Love flows better when you know Him. Life changes for the better when you know Him, with abundant blessings ready to enter your life. Now that is a thought! When you commune with God in prayer you might as well get ready to break through. You are in the right place and position.

I would not want to know anyone better than God. You need to make Him your number one priority. You can know someone with the highest education but they cannot get you into the Kingdom of Heaven. They cannot offer you salvation. They cannot bless you like Jesus does, every day. To know someone means you have to get a closer perspective of them. You may know about their family and their personal information. When you go to the doctor, he knows your organs and how to diagnose you. He knows how to treat you with the best medicine. The doctor gets intimate with your case, because it could mean life or death.

That is exactly what Jesus wants. He wants us to get to know Him intimately. People need to get to know Jesus better than knowing their spouses. Jesus will always be there in the midst of a storm. When you go through a marital storm, He is there to rescue you.

I always go back to the day that God illuminated His word for me. He made the scriptures come alive and burn in my heart. It was John 1:1-12. He came down from Heaven to live among His people and bless them.

God just loves when we want to know Him. When we take the time to fellowship with Him, we know Him better. The more you study His word, the more you get in touch with God. He is the word, according to John 1:1. In the beginning was the Word and He was with God and the Word was God. How can this be? He is God. No one can fully express all of who God is. He calls the shots. No human in society calls the shots. They may have a role but they do not call the shots. Otherwise, they would be considered false gods. No one wants that to happen, because it is an abomination to God.

When you get to know Him and the power of His resurrection and the fellowship of His suffering, you will be blessed. One thing He does is destroy demons entering into your life. In 1997, the enemy came into my house and we had a show down. I was just born again. The second time was so many years later. He came in to rise up against me and my family. He wanted everyone destroyed in my house. He also wanted my career destroyed. His plan was to get my family to hate instead of walking in peace. Peace that surpasses all understanding will guard our hearts and minds in Christ Jesus.

Get yourself a new place where you can meet God and talk to Him. Get to know your Redeemer and worship Him in the beauty of Holiness.

GOD ALREADY KNOWS

2 Corinthian 10:12-13 But they, measuring themselves by themselves, and comparing themselves among themselves, are not wise.

God is the one who knows the true measuring of a man. The mission of the believer is to help one another in love. Don't worry about trying to compare yourself with someone else or your ministry with another. . Follow Jesus' example. Embrace the gift that God gives you. You are unique. Your style is unique and powerful. There is something God requires from you. He made your ministry specifically for you. He has already measured you and knows you inside out.

A brother will help you overcome shortcomings because he is a friend. But first things first, you must ask God to remove the scales from your eyes. Matthew 6 says, remove the beam or plank from your eye so you can see yourself before judging others. Walk in humility and the anointing.

You do not have to settle for what anybody says, you should get the advice from the Holy Spirit. Your trust should always be in the Lord. He will guide your decisions for you. Trust the wisdom of God, first and foremost.

I particularly take interest in this because of the way our society has shaped itself under the enemy's umbrella. There is too much pretense by people who want to get ahead who misuse what they have for gain. I always tell my children one key statement, "Do not sell yourself to the Devil because of someone else's perception of you. They do not hold the key to heaven or hell. I am sure they really do not want to hold hell's key. It is valuable to train your children to know that they have a mind and no one should control it, except Jesus, the author and finisher.

Look to God for all your answers. Never look to see who is measuring you because they have no power to put you before the throne of God. Our Father in Heaven measures you and He knows all things about you. We serve a mighty God, who is all. He is Omnipresent, Omniscient, and Omnipotent. He is everywhere. He is the God who can tell you all about yourself. Be careful not to judge as written in Matthew 7:7.

SPIRIT MAN

GALATIONS 5: 16-21 I say then: Walk in the Spirit, and you

shall not fulfill the lust of the flesh. For the flesh lusts against the Spirit, and the Spirit against the flesh; and these are contrary to one another, so that you do not do the things that you wish. But if you are led by the Spirit, you are not under the law. Now the works of the flesh are evident, which are: adultery, fornication, uncleanness, lewdness, idolatry, sorcery, hatred, contentions, jealousies, outbursts of wrath, selfish ambitions, dissensions, heresies, envy, murders, drunkenness, revelries, and the like; of which I tell you beforehand, just as I also told *you* in time past, that those who practice such things will not inherit the kingdom of God.

There are some people who do not mind rolling in the sand . They love the dirt or the beach sand. What does sin and sand have in common? They both come in multiples and both require washing and cleansing. Sin is not your friend. Cast it off and cut it away from your life. A friend of mine told me a story about her friend. She said, it's hard finding a companion that can be true and faithful in heart with real love. She said, she and her husband both stated their vows publically and were so committed to each other and God. She said that she was so startled at what happened later that she almost lost her hope in a love lasting forever. She made it absolutely clear to me that she did not want any part of rolling in the sand.

She said, it is hard having someone you can love and they love you back 100%. She couldn't believe that her husband lied to her every night. He said one thing and did another. He said, the troops were meeting at the unit. For some strange reason, he announced it every week, at least three times a week. Well, what gave him away was that the dirt he had on his body.

She said, "My husband would leave for hours and come home covered in dirt." She wondered what would make him get so dirty. Well, one night she followed him and discovered that her husband was cheating and to cover it up he wallowed in dirt in his uniform.

I thought for a moment this must have truly hurt her. It was a good thing that she left the relationship because cheating and deception are not options. The primary needs of a relationship are love, trust, commitment, honesty, loyalty and honor. You must have Christ at the center of your relationship and nothing outside of Him.

No matter how you see it, God is watching every move of married men and married women and all single people. You do not have to roll in the sands of sin. My God is able to deliver you from all that binds you. He is able to touch the heart of anyone who is committing adultery. He loves it when you call on Him for help. Today, ask God to deliver you from all that deceives you and all evil.

I am reminded of how often people allow sin to force them to roll in the depths of sin. The good news is that you will never be able to cover it up. God is a forgiving God who can set you free.. If you are rolling in the sin of jealousy or fornication, Let God be your God today.

If the enemy wants you to roll away from God's work of witnessing to others, do not allow yourself to get caught up in it. The enemy will do his best to make you sin. God wants you to walk in the Spirit to be fruitful. God will lead you to live a victorious life regardless of what has happened in your past. It takes a truly transformed man to walk in the Spirit. This kind of man does not play with God. He reverences Him in the highest.

CHAPTER 4
GIVE GOD AN OFFERING

GEN 8:20-21 Then Noah built an altar to the Lord, and took of every clean animal and of every clean bird, and offered burnt offerings on the altar. And the Lord smelled a soothing aroma. Then the Lord said in His heart, I will never again curse the ground for man's sake, although the imagination of man's heart is evil from his youth; nor will I again destroy every living thing as I have done.

Your challenge today is to build God an altar. It only makes sense that Noah would build an ark because God directed him. When you walk with God and know Him for yourself, you will do nothing less than reverence Him in the way the Holy Spirit leads you. Please understand that Noah received the word from God to build an ark to save God's people. If you ever want to walk with God intimately, in true holiness, build an altar in your heart. Let the Lord know that your heart is open for Him to come and dwell. Give your heart over with praise and worship. God is looking for those open vessels that are seeking Him, who meditate day and night in worship. He desires to sup with those who desire to be transformed and translated like Enoch, who walked perfectly with God.

Noah built an ark to save his family and start the seed process over by being fruitful and multiplying. He did it because God recognized Noah's obedience. Noah built an altar for the Lord after the flood and this time God promised not to destroy man. God blessed future generations through Noah's obedience in the ark and the altar. Noah was God's sacrifice because his heart was clean before God. He was faithful before God and righteous before the Lord and it pleased God. So that is why God chose Noah for these tasks. Noah presented clean animals to sacrifice and offered burnt offerings to God. Noah's actions helped people to live through the power of God. However, never forget the only true sacrifice that took away the sin of the world is Jesus Christ. In Hebrews 10:5-12,

Jesus is our sacrifice for eternal life. He took away the sin of the world by the power of His love.

POSITION YOURSELF NOW!
GOD CAN FIGHT YOUR BATTLES

2 Chronicles 20:12-17 O our God, will You not judge them? For we have no power against this great multitude that is coming against us; nor do we know what to do, but our eyes *are* upon You." Now all Judah, with their little ones, their wives, and their children, stood before the LORD. Then the Spirit of the LORD came upon Jahaziel the son of Zechariah, the son of Benaiah, the son of Jeiel, the son of Mattaniah, a Levite of the sons of Asaph, in the midst of the assembly. And he said, "Listen, all you of Judah and you inhabitants of Jerusalem, and you, King Jehoshaphat! Thus says the LORD to you: 'Do not be afraid nor dismayed because of this great multitude, for the battle *is* not yours, but God's. Tomorrow go down against them. They will surely come up by the Ascent of Ziz, and you will find them at the end of the brook before the Wilderness of Jeruel. You will not *need* to fight in this *battle*. Position yourselves, stand still and see the salvation of the LORD, who is with you, O Judah and Jerusalem!' Do not fear or be dismayed; tomorrow go out against them, for the LORD *is* with you."

Position yourself and watch God move in your life. God will fight all of your battles. He always wins! Stop depending on man to fight for you. Can you remember God fighting a battle for you? Do you see anyone on your job fighting for you? It can happen; so wait on a miracle. Man might intervene with the right attitude but his power is limited. I put my mind on Jesus, the One who carries me in this lifetime and throughout eternity. I know it is God. My soul and spirit receives the answer by the power of the Holy Spirit. My friends, the answer to this process is God Himself through the precious blood of Jesus Christ.

When I think of such an experience with the Lord, I am also reminded that even through this life to the time of my funeral procession, the glory of God will still shine in my life, even as I sleep and wait on that great day of his return. This, my friend, is the confidence that we all must have, that God will carry us in all circumstances. When He returns, He will break through the sky to lift us up to be with Him forevermore. I thank God for life experiences and all of His wondrous blessings now and to come.

In my military career there were days of carrying rucksacks for quarterly 15 mile marches. I do not regret it, nor do I miss it. We had to pack it just right with the proper amount of weight and the content had to be exactly by the packing list given from the commander. It had socks, boots, clothing, and a tent inside of it along with other items. We were prepared to be survivors at any given time.

A road march taught us several things. We had to carry a big bag of stuff on our back for several hours in the dying heat. We learned discipline. We learned how to be prepared for missions to come. We learned how to lead someone through movements over rough terrains and challenging paths. We developed endurance. One thing for sure, it helped us mentally envision the possibility and probability of having to carry someone in combat or even at home.

I thank God for discipline and strength. You never know when you might have to carry someone , a buddy or even your household. If a soldier gets wounded in the heat of battle, you may have to carry that soldier to safety. You might find yourself doing what the character called, Forest Gump did. He carried several buddies to safety.

At home you might have to carry a family member or the entire family. A husband, as the priest of the house, he is obligated to take care of everyone living in his house. However, there are some things that are outside of the immediate responsibility of the priest in that house. So then the question is would you use the rucksack effect to help with things like drug addiction, teenage sexual issues, depression, financial support, religious development, and education support? I remember distinctly that it was the load that was bothering me the most. It was the weight inside the rucksack that kept forcing my straps to dig in my shoulders and arm pits causing extreme, irritating pain. I had to keep readjusting it time and time again. It made the march seem longer. I also recall that there were irritating blisters that came about during that long march. I started out with clean, non-irritated feet and returned with ugly blisters on the bottom.

JOSHUA'S VICTORY OVER KINGS

JOSHUA 10:16-30 But these five kings had fled and hidden themselves in a cave at Makkedah. And it was told Joshua, saying, "The five kings have been found hidden in the cave at Makkedah." So Joshua said, "Roll large stones against the mouth of the cave, and set men by it to guard them. And do not stay there yourselves, but pursue your enemies, and attack their rear guard. Do not allow them to enter their cities, for the LORD your God has delivered them into your hand." Then it happened, while Joshua and the children of Israel made an end of slaying them with a very great slaughter, till they had finished, that those who escaped entered fortified cities. And all the people returned to the camp, to Joshua at Makkedah, in peace. No one moved his tongue against any of the children of Israel. Then Joshua said, "Open the mouth of the cave, and bring out those five kings to me from the cave." And they did so, and brought out those five kings to him from the cave: the king of Jerusalem, the king of Hebron, the king of Jarmuth, the king of Lachish, and the king of Eglon. So it was, when they brought out those kings to Joshua, that Joshua called for all the men of Israel, and said to the captains of the men of war who went with him, "Come near, put your feet on the necks of these kings." And they drew near and put their feet on their necks. Then Joshua said to them, "Do not be afraid, nor be dismayed; be strong and of good courage, for thus the LORD will do to all your enemies against whom you fight." And afterward Joshua struck them and killed them, and hanged them on five trees; and they were hanging on the trees until evening. So it was at the time of the going down of the sun that Joshua commanded, and they took them down from the trees, cast them into the cave where they had been hidden, and laid

large stones against the cave's mouth, which remain until this very day. On that day Joshua took Makkedah, and struck it and its king with the edge of the sword. He utterly destroyed them all the people who were in it. He let none remain. He also did to the king of Makkedah as he had done to the king of Jericho. Then Joshua passed from Makkedah, and all Israel with him, to Libnah; and they fought against Libnah. And the LORD also delivered it and its king into the hand of Israel; he struck it and all the people who were in it with the edge of the sword. He let none remain in it, but did to its king as he had done to the king of Jericho

Joshua was an exceptional warrior and leader chosen by God to move his people, Israel. God wanted them to be guided as fighters and people of God. Joshua was appointed directly by God, as Moses successor. I want to use the expression, 'Joshua was a bad boy!' This is meant in the sense of greatness. His obedience revealed his manhood. Moses, through the power of God, passed the blessing on to Joshua, a humble and obedient man of God. Whatever the command spoken to Joshua by God, he would carry it out with the utmost sincerity and loyalty. It is obvious that Joshua knew God. He had full reverence. He walked in a holy commitment to God. Joshua clearly listens and acts on the words of God. In Joshua 1:9 God said, "Have I not commanded you? Be strong and of good courage; do not be afraid, nor be dismayed, for the LORD your God *is* with you wherever you go."

There would be no land, no man, nothing that could stand in the path of Joshua and bind him. God granted him victory through His word. Wherever his feet would touch, he would be victorious and God would be with him. God stated the words to Joshua again to "Be strong and of good courage; do not be afraid, nor be dismayed. It is clear that God had chosen Joshua to be a guiding light and force for His people to possess the inheritance laid up for them .

The scripture mentions that Joshua took a sword and struck the kings and buried them in a cave. All of these kings represented evil empires and territories that stood against God. They had their own gods whom they worshipped. They did not believe that God was who He said He was. Those kings and their armies were enemies to God. They clearly did not worship the Lord. The understanding here is clear, and that is God must be glorified. He is truly the victor and uses us to express His victory. The Lord has always been victorious. He never changes. The scripture is clear that "He changes not". God is still God eternal, in all power, glory and honor .

GOD CAN CHANGE ANYBODY!

ACTS 9:1-12 Then Saul, still breathing threats and murder against the disciples of the Lord, went to the high priest and asked letters from him to the synagogues of Damascus, so that if he found any who were of the Way, whether men or women, he might bring them bound to Jerusalem. As he journeyed he came near Damascus, and suddenly a light shone around him from heaven. Then he fell to the ground, and heard a voice saying to him, "Saul, Saul, why are you persecuting Me?" And he said, "Who are You, Lord?"Then the Lord said, "I am Jesus, whom you are persecuting. It *is* hard for you to kick against the goads." So he, trembling and astonished, said, "Lord, what do You want me to do?" Then the Lord *said* to him, "Arise and go into the city, and you will be told what you must do." And the men who journeyed with him stood speechless, hearing a voice but seeing no one. Then Saul arose from the ground, and when his eyes were opened he saw no one. But they led him by the hand and brought *him* into Damascus. And he was three days without sight, and neither ate nor drank. Now there was a certain disciple at Damascus named Ananias; and to him the Lord said in a vision, "Ananias." And he said, "Here I am, Lord." So the Lord *said* to him, "Arise and go to the street called Straight, and inquire at the house of Judas for *one* called Saul of Tarsus, for behold, he is praying. And in a vision he has seen a man named Ananias coming in and putting *his* hand on him, so that he might receive his sight."

There are many soldiers that have gone to war and had to do some of the ugliest and evil acts on this planet. Now these same people need help in life. You are never too far for Jesus to reach you. Some people think that God is too distant to forgive them. God can change anybody! You just need to let it go and surrender to the King of kings, Lord of lords. Make Him your Lord. Do not miss out on this!!

The Apostle Paul experienced his conversion by Jesus Christ, while traveling on the road to Damascus with the intent to kill Christians. He hated Christians. Next time you find yourself traveling somewhere to do evil, make sure you understand that God is watching. You just might be the next person to experience a conversion. You should be converted anyway because of the love of God. God can use all saints. Believe the Apostles, Prophets, Evangelist, Pastors, and Teachers as described in Ephesians 4:11 which are those who operate in the five-fold ministry, God is calling for people to be converted and use their gifts. If you feel that you are lost, you need to experience a touch of Jesus that will change your life forever. Please understand that no one is exempt from His touch to fulfill the purpose He has set for each person.

The Apostle Paul's life was converted by the touch of Jesus who saw Saul on the road to destruction. Everyone needs a touch because of the sin that creeps in and reigns over our lives. We need His touch every day because we fall short of His glory. We need His touch because we all have been persecutors and violators of the faith in Christ, in some form or fashion. However, He is forever forgiving. He always delivers us from our weaknesses and sins. We do not have to act all cute and prestigious and set in our ways. You see, everyone has something broken that will require God's attention. The only one who can fix it is Jesus. Whatever it takes for God to do a new thing in your life, whether it is conversion or a blessing, ask God to do it and do it now. The enemy wants to stop you in your tracks, but God wants you to prosper in His Kingdom. You have a purpose in Christ. Your purpose means more to the Lord than to the enemy because God sees you as one of His. The enemy is just a deterrent. He has a goal to make you turn your back on Jesus. But Jesus has all eternal power that is instantly manifested in your life for His Kingdom purpose.

It is important to start this lesson out giving the essential makeup of blessings and being able to explain the necessity of sight in the spiritual realm. It is much needed and has been avoided too long. Sometimes people cringe at the fact that there is a spiritual realm and two different spirits looking at you and both forces existing for different purposes.

God desires to bless you and curse those who curse you. The enemy simply comes to steal, kill and destroy. The question to you today is which one do you chose? I am sure you made the right choice today. If you have salvation in Jesus Christ, you want the spiritual realm to see what the Lord wants to reveal to you.

One of the most effective parts of Jesus ministry was the demonstration of restoring sight. Jesus is the only one who can restore and give sight. There is no other. So do not be fooled by the enemy. Jesus dealt with a blind man who needed sight because he was born with a birth defect from his mother's womb. He dealt with religious leaders who were confused about the new birth. They had no vision and no concept of being born again. Their sights were limited by their spiritual conditions. Jesus made it very clear that you must be born again. They were too blind to understand and to see that the Son of God was in the midst of them, healing and revealing His gracious loving kindness. They were too caught up with the law, rather than the truth standing before their very eyes. They had different interpretations of the identity of Jesus.

God wanted to restore life to people.. God is no respecter of persons. He reigns on the just as well as the unjust. Jesus restored people for more than one reason. His primary reason for restoring is love. He loves us more than a parent can. It was the demonstration of love in Him. He sees all things and we ourselves see nothing without the blessing of spiritual sight. God has been protecting us.

Christians have a unique lifestyle that must be projected and demonstrated at all times. People watch to see if you are setting an example in your walk. They want to know if you act like a Christian, demonstrating the love that Jesus gives. They want to know that you are filled with the Holy Ghost. So then show them that you are filled in the Spirit of Christ. Draw them to Christ under the power of God. Use what you have to draw them. When the Apostle was drawn in, he spent the remainder of his life drawing people to the Lord. In fact, that became his mission for Christ. He was a chosen vessel. When God removes your scales in the spirit, then you will see and become effective witnesses in Christ Jesus.

When we expect to see things, we must be patient that God will reveal the blessing in time. Count on your spiritual sight. The Apostle Paul said, 2 Corinthians 4:18 while we do not look at the things which are seen, but at the things which are not seen. For the things which are seen *are* temporary, but the things which are not seen *are* eternal. I believe that once God changed Paul, he could adopt this passage under the anointing. We see to get the blessings and be obedient to His will and commands.

CRUCIFIED FOR ME AND YOU!

JOHN 19:31-37 Therefore, because it was the Preparation Day, that the bodies should not remain on the cross on the Sabbath (for that Sabbath was a high day), the Jews asked Pilate that their legs might be broken, and that they might be taken away. Then the soldiers came and broke the legs of the first and of the other who was crucified with Him. But when they came to Jesus and saw that He was already dead, they did not break His legs. But one of the soldiers pierced His side with a spear, and immediately blood and water came out. And he who has seen has testified, and his testimony is true; and he knows that he is telling the truth, so that you may believe. For these things were done that the Scripture should be fulfilled, "Not one of His bones shall be broken." And again another Scripture says, "They shall look on Him whom they pierced".

Surely the death of Jesus had an impact in the lives of millions of people because He took on all the pain and suffering in His body. The blood has impacted every life on earth and all that God intended. He is the God of restoration and salvation, setting people free! He was crucified for us to have life and have it more abundantly, above all, eternal life. God loves His people so much that we have Jesus' DNA in us. With DNA, you can track down what family you are in. It will be easy to track me down because I have the makeup of Jesus in me.

One of the first accounts in the Bible regarding blood issues was in the case surrounding Can and Abel. Cain slew his brother Abel. Cain killed his brother because he was jealous over the sacrifice that Abel had presented before God. Abel's sacrifice pleased God. Cain did not please God with His sacrifice of fruit. Do not misunderstand and think that fruit is not good, because on the contrary it is good. It was not the perfect sacrifice that God was looking for, He was looking for obedience. The sacrifice had to have blood involved in it. Abel pleased God with the sacrifice of meat. He was the keeper of sheep. Meat is the reflection of the Lamb that would be slain someday for all of Israel, God's people and the lost. The lamb would be the perfect sacrifice because the lamb had to be slain so blood would have to be spilled. This would be a picture of Jesus Christ, the Lamb who was slain for the remission of sin.

The fruit that Cain presented to God was good but it could not serve as a sacrifice. It did have its connection to the garden because the garden was filled with fruit and God had blessed everything. At the same time, God is looking for your best offering. What you give is noticed by the Lord. Do not allow sin to take your best offering away from God. The enemy specializes in provoking people into a sin-filled lifestyle.

During that particular time, sin had run its course and reflected on the first family. Whenever a family has been blessed, you need to understand that the enemy will do everything in his power to destroy that family. We are dealing with a force that has been defeated. However, this enemy still chooses to raise his ugly head, thinking that he has power to defeat you. Thank God that He is our refuge and strong tower. He covers us in His blood.

Scientists made a breakthrough discovery about DNA, the breakdown in identity of our individual blood. They use DNA to investigate crimes. Investigators can know exactly who the person is that left the blood at the crime scene. They know who to track down. They can match the DNA to a full description of the violator. They trace different factors and characteristics about the

DNA in different people. They can do it for humans and animals. They know your blood type.

I was in the hospital years ago. I understood that my blood was my life line. I knew that if my blood was in trouble with diseases or anything, I would be in trouble. God gives us wisdom to take care of our blood systems with vitamins and a proper diet. Because God supplies my need, I came out of the hospital in the best of health.

God has the people to know and to see things both spiritually and naturally. Abel's blood was on the ground and he was innocent. God could hear the blood crying from the ground. Cain was scared and did not want to tell the truth, but God already knew. He already knew the circumstance surrounding the killing of his brother. He knew Cain had struck his brother because he was jealous of an offering.

The blood of Jesus Christ is applied to the hearts of those who believe. They must know that the blood is what saves us from being destroyed by God's wrath.

We are reminded of the many wars that were fought and blood was shed for freedom and peace. Some people are moved by that fact. As a result of those wars, God saw our relatives through. He is still protecting us now and bringing us through the wars that we have with principalities, demons and all of our enemies. God is all merciful and graceful in offering us His protection.

Today we live because the blood of Jesus was applied over our lives. He covers our heart, mind, soul, spirit and strengthens us. He enables us to be victorious against Satan in every way. Satan was defeated by Jesus because of His love demonstrated on the cross and the power in His blood applied. He covers all of us, the lost and those who feel abandoned. He covers us because He loves us more than we love ourselves. His love transcends imaginations. He paid our debt to the Father. Because of His love for us, He washed us whiter than snow. He removed the sin stain. Isaiah 64. Thanks be to the living God who has delivered us from darkness and the grip of sin.

Anybody can apply almost anything in life. Jesus is our cure anyway you want to see it. Any application outside the will of God will be useless because it is limited and it does not have the power of Christ in it. But the application of His word will bless us throughout eternity.

Money is our purchasing power. Some make it their essential substance of life. That is so far from the truth. There is nothing more powerful than the blood of the Lamb applied to our lives. There is nothing that can be compared to the precious blood of the Lamb. Money and power will not fix your spiritual life. Winning the lottery will not fix your soul or offer salvation. There is nothing wrong with having money. But we need to understand that Jesus died to give us life and give it more abundantly. He has made all things possible for us. So it really does not matter whatever else you apply in your life outside of the precious blood. The blood is the only thing that can save you. Today is your day to accept the Jesus Christ as the Lord of your life.

Rich people put millions of dollars on Wall Street into the stock market and into banks. Nevertheless, there are millions of dollars to renew investments every day. Some would debate that these millions do not mean anything. I want to say to you that God has a blessing for you. Do not get discouraged. Just remember, do not let Jesus pass you. Instead grab hold of Him and get your blessings. Make Jesus the investment in your life from now on. He made you His! He washed you in His precious blood to atone us from the wrath of God and the grip of the enemy. Remember, you are covered in His blood and you are rich in His kingdom. You can't help but to be highly blessed.

Governments allocate billions of dollars each month for war and foreign policy. They invest to maintain relationships and peace. They invest and use top dollars to bring wars to a close and find peaceful solutions. Why not invest in Him who loves to bring peace to our hearts and minds. Invest in His Kingdom, by first accepting Him in your life.

Jesus defeated Satan on Calvary for the world to come back to Him as He took away the sin. His blood was our atonement. He identifies with us and His blood. Someone once jokingly asked "Who had made him clean through and through? He wanted to see the evidence of who cleaned him. He wanted to know how the blood was applied. God is able to do all of these things. Somehow in His own infinite wisdom, He broke us out of the prison of Satan and allowed us to sup with Him. You can be transformed by the renewing of you mind.

The blood applied is your way in to get to heaven and bow before His throne. He knows each of us by name. He knows the impact of His blood. We know that He is the God that blessed through the power of His blood.

We take communion now to recognize His blood and broken body. Corinthians 11:23-34. We identify with His death burial, resurrection, and return.

It appears that in order to get something to happen new something to be victorious, there always has to be blood involved. I am so glad that Jesus was made the perfect sacrifice for my sin. He became sin on a cross for all my transgressions, all of my mistakes, all of my failures in loving other people. He became the one and only perfect sacrifice. His bloodshed was and is the perfect purpose and means of new life. Jesus is the one who made life possible to live and worth living.

HE DEMONSTRATED LOVE LIKE NO OTHER!

JOHN 19:31-35 Therefore, because it was the Preparation Day, that the bodies should not remain on the cross on the Sabbath (for that Sabbath was a high day), the Jews asked Pilate that their legs might be broken, and that they might be taken away. Then the soldiers came and broke the legs of the first and of the other who was crucified with Him. But when they came to Jesus and saw that He was already dead, they did not break His legs. But one of the soldiers pierced His side with a spear, and immediately blood and water came out. And he who has seen has testified, and his testimony is true; and he knows that he is telling the truth, so that you may believe.

That day was the day that every man, woman and child should never forget. This was the day that love was demonstrated beyond measure. No other event in history and in our minds can compare. This is the most critical event that could have taken place on earth.

Jesus was put to death for me and you. People cry when they think of the fact that one man fully divine, innocent of every charge that was place against Him, took a beating that no one could ever have made it through. People cry when they think of the fact that He loves us and was willing to hang on a cross for us.

My heart still tries to imagine how He could love me so, in that he was willing to carry His own cross while being beaten. Then He allowed Himself to be nailed to a cross constructed by evil men. I still continue trying to imagine the fullness of His love for me to take on my sin, a person He created before time. In Isaiah 53, it is written, "by His stripes we are healed." We were on our way to death having the wrath of God poured out on us. He already recognized us as a wretched people, yet precious in His eyes. But Jesus stepped in and saved us. The cross is precious. Jesus carried it and died for our sin. In those times, they hung criminals on the cross and waited for them to suffocate. They nailed Him to the cross and pierced Him in the side and blood came out with water.

We know that Jesus is precious in our heart for what He has done. When we see the cross, we see the most precious commitment to love that has ever existed in this world. He died for you and me. When people truly receive the truth in their hearts that is when change comes forth. Worship and heartfelt thanksgiving is activated on the inside. Some people wear a cross as a symbol and a reminder of what Jesus did for a world entrenched in sin. God redeemed his people. God destroyed sin in His son's body on the cross. There is simply no sacrifice that could take the place of Jesus. He was and is the only way out of sin. He is the only way to everlasting life. Jesus is the way the truth and the life and He is the only way to the Father.

HOW I MADE IT OVER! WORSHIP HIM!

REVELATION 7:13 Then one of the elders asked me, These in the white robes who are they, and where did they come? I answered, Sir, you know. And he said, These are they who have come out of the great tribulation; they have washed their robes and made them white in the blood of the Lamb.

Nothing will be more fulfilling until we saints can say, "How I made it over". We made it over by grace, mercy and the love of Jesus Christ. Examine closely the scripture above. Can you imagine the excitement and joy in John's heart? If the heart could shed tears, his tears would have overflowed in heaven. Either way, he needed a way to cry because of the goodness of God. I know I made it over by the power of God. I made it over because God carried me. I made it over because in my weakness, I have his strength. I know who to call on to lend me a helping hand. I made it over when I left my past behind and joined the Jesus' club. No more having people shooting at me in a night club.

John had a vision that allowed him to see in the heavenly realm. In fact, he was taken to heaven in the Spirit to see what God wanted to reveal to him. In that event, John was moved in the spirit, in a time portal. He was allowed to see those dressed in white robes. Jesus even showed John Himself. He revealed the throne to John. He revealed the fountain of blood that never runs dry. He revealed what would take place in the future to John. In one scene, one of the elders in heaven saw John and responded to him. The Elder had identified the thousands and thousands of worshipers as those that came out of the great tribulation.

God blessed all worshipers in that He allowed their robes to be washed in the blood of the Lamb. These are those that believe and have accepted Christ Jesus as Lord and Savior. They made it through the roughest of tests by faith. There is no one else that can make robes white by the washing of the blood. Our Father in Heaven can do things beyond our comprehension and our wildest imaginations.

God wants His people to see where they will spend eternity when they become one of His followers. God wants His children to see the blessing of eternal life. It is the will of God that we spend eternity with Him. His will is for you to join Him in Heaven when the time comes. So believe in Him and worship Him and be watchful for when He breaks the sky wide open. Life will no longer be as you know it. He is Lord!

Our white robes are not ordinary robes. We wear robes for so many reasons. Some are for walking around in the comfort of your home. Some robes represent those that fight in the boxing arenas. There are robes that are specifically designed for priests. We have been designated to wear robes that represent priesthood. Jesus wore His robe and it was designed perfectly to fit our High Priest. You can worship in any attire, but the white robe that Jesus will place on us is to recognize and set apart those that made it through the tribulation. They are anchored in praise for the Most High God. Today is your day to know for sure that you will wear a white robe that was washed in the blood of the Lamb. Get God today and worship Him in the beauty of His holiness.

Please understand that the Lord washed those that followed Him and gave them a new identity in heaven. When the Lord gives you a new identity, it's time to act on it and use what you have from the Lord. Ask God to anoint you for His purpose.

Most people have an identity crisis that plague their lives. Today is a new day and the old day has passed away. It is high time for you to get your blessings. Look for your blessings that will get you to heaven.

When all the Christians get to heaven, they will have a joyous time in worship and in praising His righteous name. There will be a continuous party in heaven. It will last forever, because there is everlasting rejoicing in worshipping God. There is joy in His presence. So, can you imagine those that are destined to come out of the great tribulation? Those that are conquers in Jesus Christ will come out of the great tribulation. He said, in Romans that we are more than conquerors in Christ Jesus.

I believe it to be absolutely true because His word in Rev 7:17 says that "For the Lamb on the throne will be their shepherd. He will lead them to springs of life-giving water. And God will wipe every tear from their eye." These believers will come out of the tribulation. You see when you worship and serve the Lord in faithfulness, He will bless you to the point of bringing you out of the tribulation to get your white robe and worship him. Then you will reign with Him forever. Praise to His Holy name!

THE POWER OF WISDOM

Proverbs 9:1 Wisdom has built her house, She has hewn out her seven pillars.

Wisdom is the key in establishing a house. God's wisdom established His house as the Holy Place to dwell in. We are invited to come to the banquet prepared for us. Of course, Jesus must take first place in our lives. We must honor him at home and as we serve Him. The seven pillars are representative of the splendor of the house God has built. Seven signifies the sacredness of the word of God.

The first level of ministry starts at home with your family. Use your home to train your family in the word and power of God. Do you want your household to be complete in Jesus Christ? Do you want to ask God to restore and bless your house so it is pleasing in His sight? Wisdom leads the man of the house. Ask God to do a cleaning through your house. Ask God to keep His anointing in your body and your home. Ask God to take over. Do not leave it unattended to just run to church. Do not leave it out of order. Church needs to start in the home. Take your concerns to the altar in your house. You can also take it to church to see your priest and bow at that altar. Nevertheless family matters start at home. Do not just leave your house just hanging. Why should I minister somewhere else before nurturing my family? Keep the focus on the family once you have taken it to the Lord.

Your very first step is to become a man and woman of God for His purpose. Once you have done that then focus on your family with even greater vigor. Seek God to help increase your faith. Start your practice at home and watch how the Lord moves in your life. This does not mean forget correcting your children. In fact teaching, correcting and nourishing them is a ministry itself. Start at home with love and kindness.

Wisdom extends beyond ordinary knowledge. This scripture points to the fact that wisdom lacks nothing. It represents completeness in the will of God. It is God's business for Him to complete what He purposed for life. He does not leave anything undone. When He acts He blesses us in tremendous ways that we can never repay or even imagine. This wisdom in your house should reveal a house that is working on complete happiness and joy. Wisdom is also a way of saying, you are acting in perfection to satisfy your house. God's house is still His house. But you need to know that He is able to recover you and bless you in your house.

A well respected and friendly couple fought like cats and dogs, always at each other's throats. They were all about impressing someone else and full of excuses as to why the marriage was not working. It got so bad that they took each other to court. But you need to understand that God can show up in any court room and can change the heart of everyone involved, including the judge. God has wisdom that He gives the judge. The Lord can even give you wisdom in the court room. He can reconcile your marriage before you get to that point. You need to develop a sense of trusting the Most High God and developing a heart of wisdom.

A good woman who is in love with Jesus will demonstrate love and wisdom. She will make it work because she is responsible for her house. She will reveal the attitude of a helper or helpmate to her husband as Eve did in Genesis. More importantly, she learns to submit and surrender to Jesus completely. When doing so, her character changes for the good of the family and the ministry that God has for her.

Anytime a person has to deal with sin, God will immediately restore. He wants you in His kingdom. You need wisdom so that you will not punish yourself with self-guilt and self-denial. God helps you to look up to the hills from whence cometh your help. God's wisdom will carry you over and help you to live in the blessings. James 3

OVERCOME YOUR PRIDE

PROVERBS 6:16 These six things the Lord hates, Yes, seven are an abomination to Him: A proud look, A lying tongue, Hands that shed innocent blood, A heart that devises wicked plans, Feet that are swift in running to evil, A false witness who speaks lies, And one who sows discord among brethren. My son, keep your father's command, And do not forsake the

law of your mother. Bind them continually upon your heart;

When people learn the power of love, it helps to overcome the power of hate. As long as people keep their minds on the Lord instead of meditating and entertaining evil, then their blessings will be released. God is warning us to not walk in pride, hate or any manner of evil. Walk in love so that you will win souls. Walk under the influence of the Holy Spirit so that hate will not grip you.

God wants us to know the seven things that He hates. He wants us to keep our focus on His loving kindness and His character. Listen to what God is saying get wisdom to overcome. God doesn't like a proud look that makes you feel like you are above Him. He is saying don't just concentrate on your image. Know who made you by speaking a word. He wants to remind us that our eyes are important because of how we see ourselves. In some cases, people see themselves higher than God.

I was in a group study which covered different aspects of being a good employee in an environment that supported wounded soldiers. In the class, they emphasized goals. We normally make goals to remind us of the individual achievements we want to make. I believe that if you replace negatives with positives; then replace evil with good, then you will be able to make an impact.

Try something like this for breaking a proud look: Keep your eyes on the Lord and not your own accomplishments or what you think that you achieved by yourself. Do not lie on others because it is sinful and God sees it rolling off of the tongues of the person telling the lie and the hurt it causes the innocent. Don't murder or take the life of anyone because it is not the will of God that you live with such pain and regret. It is not the will of God that you shed innocent blood. God is able to deliver you out of any situation the enemy lures you into. Keep your heart filled in the Spirit of Jesus Christ. If you have Jesus inside your heart, then wicked schemes cannot take root because you are now rooted in the will of God by His Son. Remember the story of Moses and Pharaoh. His heart was hardened for the purpose of God by pouring out evil upon the children of Israel. God finally penetrated his heart and convinced him at the Red Sea. But it took God having to drown

Pharaoh's army. God does not want us to run to evil and celebrate evil. That is what happens when the mind is on worldly things. Do not become a false witness that tells feel-good stories that are really lies. Whatever you do, "follow peace with all men because without it, no man shall see God."

THE POWER OF OBEDIENCE

Romans 5:19 For as by one man's disobedience many were made sinners, so also by one Man's obedience many will be made righteous.

One man's obedience has covered my life. When you begin to walk in righteousness because you made a decision to subject yourself to the will of God, the Holy Spirit will bless you in a tremendous way. God wants us to be obedient and submit to His authority and purpose for our lives in every way. We must not submit partially, but completely. It is the power of the Holy Spirit that enables us in obedience and reveals to the Father our commitment to Him. Obedience enables us to be true worshipers and honor Him in the Spirit. Our Lord makes us righteous by our conversion. With Christ in our hearts and minds, we are renewed beings that walk in the spirit. The Lord takes hold of us and keeps us from being overcome by evil plots, manipulation and the grip of sin. Having been made righteous, we begin to reap the harvest because of our obedience. The righteous will live for the uplifting of the Kingdom of God. Therefore our lives are ordered by the Lord.

God will show His people His blessings in greater abundance if we abide in Him with obedience. His blessings flow more and more in our lives, because we believe in the power of His word, His will and promises through the scriptures. It is amazing how people still avoid the most fundamental requirement of God. God spells it out in so many scriptures and in so many ways. The first thing in pleasing God is obedience. Why? It is because obedience demonstrates individual love for God. He loves us as well. Obedience is top priority in pleasing God. The Holy Spirit helps us to be validated in God's eyes with these types of spiritual traits.

It is because He said "love the Lord with all your heart and your entire mind and all your strength." Obedience is necessary to have order and everything that follows for the glorification of Him who called us out of darkness. Walking in the Spirit of the Lord will enable you to be obedient and worship Him with all your heart. Your walk will become faithful and life will be better because he will become real in your life, like never before. Anything on the outside is not of God and has no bearing in your praise life. You will become one who walks with praise on your lips and in the depths of your heart. You will be the one who worships in total admiration and glory to His righteous name. This will be because now you know Him.

There is an order that no man can stop from God. Man is incapable of stopping your servant heart. Man is incapable of stopping your heart of stewardship. Man is incapable of stopping the anointing on your life. Once God ordains it, man just needs to say Lord what do you want me to do? How can I serve to glorify you Lord? Otherwise man will think that He is God.

There is an order in the home. The man must be the priest in your house or else you are open to the gateway of hell. If a wife is not submissive to her husband then the house is out of order. She is blocking those multiple blessings that God set to overflow in her life.

Then there is the seed planter in the house. God gave man the ability to plant seed. He gave man the right to plant seed so that He would raise an heir in his house. You can look at Abraham's story and see that the blessings on Abraham were significant. God had already planned on giving Abraham a son and heir. This simply means that God was waiting on Abraham to be obedient in faith and at the same time, God wanted Abraham to trust Him.

One of the things that I learned about God is that if you trust Him and wait on His promises, you are in for the blessings of a lifetime. He will not let you down. He will cause you to overflow in blessings. He never goes against His promises. Not only will you be blessed, your entire household will be blessed. I am telling you, right now, that it is time to completely trust God for order. Walk in the power of faith that God will fulfill your heart's desires.

God still orders the house in other respects. You remember God giving Adam a woman. He gave him a woman in holy matrimony, a sealed marriage. Adam was so powerful that he announced that this woman 'is bone of my bone and flesh of my flesh'. Adam was signifying that they were one under God in marriage. God did not stop there. He gave the woman the ability to give birth. There is no other human being with that capability. Then Jesus said that every male that comes forth from a woman's womb is blessed. Jeremiah 1:5. I just wanted to tell you that the birth process is never over. The purpose is to bruise the head of the serpent while the Lord is still blessing us. It was the Lord who gave this gift to women.

CHAPTER 5
I AM MY BROTHER'S KEEPER

GENESIS 4:1-11 Now Adam knew Eve his wife, and she conceived and bore Cain, and said, "I have acquired a man from the LORD." Then she bore again, this time his brother Abel. Now Abel was a keeper of sheep, but Cain was a tiller of the ground. And in the process of time it came to pass that Cain brought an offering of the fruit of the ground to the LORD. Abel also brought of the firstborn of his flock and of their fat. And the LORD respected Abel and his offering, but He did not respect Cain and his offering. And Cain was very angry, and his countenance fell. So the LORD said to Cain, "Why are you angry? And why has your countenance fallen? If you do well, will you not be accepted? And if you do not do well, sin lies at the door. And its desire *is* for you, but you should rule over it." Now Cain talked with Abel his brother; and it came to pass, when they were in the field, that Cain rose up against Abel his brother and killed him. Then the LORD said to Cain, "Where *is* Abel your brother?" He said, "I do not know. *Am* I my brother's keeper?" And He said, "What have you done? The voice of your brother's blood cries out to Me from the ground.

Conception happens and brothers are birthed from their mother's womb. They had the same blood line. Therefore they were blood brothers. Most of us have heard the saying that blood is thicker than water. His blood ties us altogether in Jesus Christ. His blood washed us, therefore we share the living Savior.

Brothers must always stick together. In my family, I am my brother's keeper. I will step right in to fight the enemy off of my brother instantly, without hesitation. Why? We fight together because he is my blood brother and my daddy taught us right. We were made to fight for our brothers. In the Christian world, we fight for our brothers. You just don't stand there and let a devil beat your Christian brother down!

Family is the core of our society with Jesus Christ as the head of our lives and families. Many families may appear perfect on the outside, which may be a cover up or an illusion. Façade is the real word because it means to cover up ugly and appear perfect; or appear to have everything in order. But God sees right through it. There are many other people that see right through it as well. Don't put on a façade with God, or with family and friends. One of the main reasons that sin lies at the door is that God made family so precious in His sight. Since family is important to God, it is crucial in each one of our lives. The family unit gives a comforting sense of belonging to people who love you. We mess up from time to time, but the fact remains we need our families and we need God to lead each person in the family.

You know how it is when you see a television show that projects the images of a loving family. It makes your heart warm and you want to act better. You want that real connection and power of love with your family. For starters, call your family on the phone, visit and let them know that they are special and loved by you.

One of the most important points of the family is the role each sibling plays in each other's life. Everyone is a keeper of the rest of the family. So stop feeling like you are the lost sheep of the family or the one designated to do everything. If it happens, let the rest of them know, you all have to work together. Ask the Holy Spirit to lift your spirit. He will do it. So trust Him in all things. Trust Him to lead the family.

God puts us in positions, something we do not expect. You may have to take hold of the situation in your family and lead. God already knows best for you. He might just be calling you to lead them in some ways. But when we remember Mother and her love, it gets us back on track. We need to be reminded of how to survive as family members.

The family must be focused. Family members must be introduced to Jesus as Lord and Savior. There will be more confusion if you do not have Christ as the center of your life. Families simply need Him as the center. Leadership comes from God and the appointed priest of the house. Wives, help him lead the family. Build him up to help you and the babies. God will recognize that order is forming in your house. When you begin to focus on Jesus as the center of your life, then you will come to a point where you are pleasing God. He loves it when we give Him all the glory. Focusing on your family, as it was originally intended for Adam and Eve, is the goal. Do not shift blame to one another. God is not looking for you to play the blame game. He is the One who can judge all things. Your blame game does not have any weight in Jesus Christ. It is only the enemy starting confusion and trying to lead you to the pits of hell. Immediately go into prayer and ask the Lord to rebuke all enemy attacks. There is no weight too heavy for God. He lifts weights every day. What makes you think that your small weight between you, a sibling or a friend is too heavy for God? The answer is nothing is too heavy for God. Call on the Lord and watch Him mesmerize you and your family with His power.

Take life with your brother serious. Love him more by giving him the word. It is the key. Jesus Himself offers the greatest gift that you can receive, salvation through His word and His power. Family matters because of the blood of Jesus that washes us white as snow.

KNOCK ON GOD'S HEAVENLY DOOR!

MATTHEW 7:7 Ask, and it will be given to you; seek, and you will find; knock, and it will be opened to you. For everyone who asks receives, and he who seeks finds, and to him who knocks it will be opened.

If someone knocks on your front door, they get your full attention. Then you get up and open the door for them to enter. Surely you would get up and let them in. It is human nature to be nice to people. Since it was so easy letting them in, what are you going to do when God knocks at your heart? Romans 10:9 help us to confess and walk people into salvation. He wants to get inside your heart today! He wants to give you a transformed heart and salvation. Every time you get an opportunity to open your heart to

God, do it and see what happens. He will fill your heart with joy, salvation and multiple blessings. He will speak to your heart and give you marvelous revelation knowledge. He will speak directly from heaven into your heart. Every time you hear God speaking to your heart, allow Him to do a work on the inside of you. It is important to understand that God is always working on the heart of man. The Holy Spirit is always at work in the lives of both the believer and the unbeliever. He wants to convince the unbeliever who Jesus is and what the advantages are to surrendering to Him as Lord.

The question you have to ask yourself is what do you want in life? Jesus can help you with anything. Have you asked Him a question about your situation? He said ask, and it will be given to you. He did not limit anything because He already knows what you will ask. Maybe one good idea is to ask God to help you accomplish your dreams and reach your destiny. If you ask and believe, then you need to trust Him. Faith in God is the solution to that thing you ask of God. If you ask God for a new house because you need it, the God we are talking about supplies all of your need. If you need your marriage to work because of distractions and enemy attacks, God is the One that puts marriages together in Corinthians 7. He will work on your union according to His purpose.

Seek after God always because He is first in your life. If you had challenges or barriers in the past, make Him first. If you are searching for the Spirit of God in your life, make sure that you have accepted Him into your heart first. Some people believe that God is just with them. The Bible declares that God saves us by His grace in Ephesians 2:8. When you know that you have been saved by grace, seeking Him is always in the forefront of your mind because you know that God hears and will answer you. Why are you seeking God? You seek God because you need Him to bless you. You seek God because you need someone to trust completely and with total authority and confidentiality. You need to seek God because your life depends on it. You see the Bible declares that the enemy comes to kill, steal and destroy. He is like a roaring lion seeking and roaming this earth to see whom he may devour. The scripture says in Psalms 27, that the Lord is my strength and my salvation who shall I fear. The Lord is the strength of my life whom shall I be afraid? The power of His love is what saves us every time. Seek Him with all your heart. Isaiah says seek Him while He may be found. Today is your day to know Him better.

God is always knocking at the heart of man. He is knocking at the door of your heart to come in and stay with you. You, just like everyone else, have an entrance in your heart that God can come in and sup with you. He will come in and change your heart and transform you into the image of the person He wants you to be.

Yes, God is just like that mail man knocking at your door to give you new mail in which you receive that $10,000 dollar check. Start thinking like that! If someone opens a door for you to become a millionaire, an actor, song artist, dancer, receive it because you believe that you deserve it. Well that is what Jesus is saying; you deserve the best, at all times. You deserve to have Jesus in your heart. He is knocking to come into your heart. In Romans 10:9, the Apostle writes "that if you confess with your mouth the Lord Jesus and believe in your heart that God has raised Him from the dead, you will be saved." He is more important than all other opportunities and things that you have acquired in a life time. In fact, he is the reason for those material blessings and success.

MAKE THE RIGHT DECISION

GENESIS 12:1-3 Now the LORD had said to Abram: "Get out of your country, From your family And from your father's house, To a land that I will show you. I will make you a great nation; I will bless you And make your name great; And you shall be a blessing. I will bless those who bless you, And I will curse him who curses you; And in you all the families of the earth shall be blessed."

When He speaks to us about taking specific steps in life, we must be ready to obey and please Him. The Lord our God is always looking out for us. God might be telling you to step out of your comfort zone, step out of your condition into a new level of faith. God wants you to step out and never let anyone stunt your growth. You need to believe God and do it! The questions for you are: Do you hear His voice? Will you obey Him to get your blessings? Then glorify Him? The answer for you and I should be a resounding yes Lord, I will obey. I will step out by faith. I will make a decision right now to serve you.

Abram heard God's voice and moved by faith and obedience. God wanted Abram to move because on the other end would be abundance of blessings. You must move when God calls you for a mission. There will be so many blessings, that you will not be able to count. He is not looking for your perfection. He is looking for you to make the right decision to move when He directs. It is our destiny to act in faith and accordingly when God speaks. He already knows! Nothing is a surprise to God, our Father. Stepping out of your condition to get your blessing is one of God's priorities for your life. The top priority is acting in faith and obedience. The priority is to first get salvation. The simple step of opening your mouth in confession and opening your heart is a form of stepping out of your condition. Ask Jesus to come into your heart today. Then your faith walk will begin.

Abram was later rewarded for his faith and obedience in God. One of the things that impressed God so much was Abram's faith to say goodbye to any opposition in his life, all obstacles, intimidations and bondage. Abram was not allowing false gods and any such thing related to it to stop him. He believed in God. His faith was strong and genuine. God loved that about Abram. He did not allow any relative stop him. You have to make a decision to not allow family members or anyone to hold you back. They may not have had the kind of experience with God as you. You have been transformed to walk in the image of Jesus Christ. You are born again.

Sometimes in life you have to strip yourself of things that are holding you back. Other people may not understand what is going on with you. But you need to know for yourself what God has for you. God has for you what God has for you. No one can take it away. They may not understand what you are experiencing in Christ; and that is fine. They might not understand the joy you feel in your heart because you heard God speaking to you. They just don't know what you are experiencing! They may never know. Take the nearest exit route to get away from what is holding you back. God wants His people to develop an attitude of stepping out in faith and on His word. His word is your path of life. His word will deliver you and enable you to prosper.

You may have heard plenty people talking about stepping out. The problem is they develop the when, where, why and how are you going to do it mentality. Those questions are fine but if you use them to make an excuse, then you will miss out on the blessings God has for you. We need to get out of the picture of self -glorification and give God the glory. Do not misunderstand, you may have to do some things to get thing going. But you must operate under God's influence. If you are going to do anything that will succeed, you need to do it because of God and under the power of the Holy Spirit. Your moment and timing and intention must be because of God. Abram strictly moved because of God. By reading this scripture it tells me that Abram had to have a heart to move strictly for God's purpose. One thing for sure is that when you step out and obey God, there are blessings in store.

I look at many of the churches today and most of them stepped out when there seemed to be no hope and no help from anyone else. But they trusted in God. You are not going into any ministry without trusting and having faith in God. People have started small ministries to mega ministries and the attack still goes on against the church. But the ministry continues in the power of His might.

I believe God sees the worship inside us and that worship belongs to Him. God sees the faith inside of us and that faith belongs to Him. God sees the glory that you have to give Him. It is not ours, not one measure is yours or mine, and it belongs to our Lord, the Redeemer of our souls.

Today, I want you to know that your obedience and faith in Christ Jesus is far better than any prophet or any other person in the Bible. We need to have the hope in Jesus' return just like we have to believe in His resurrection from the dead. You see, my friend, Jesus moved by faith when He carried the cross on Cavalry. He did so that we could one day see that His faith in His Father was stronger than even Abram's when He moved in accordance to the voice of the Lord.

I remember the days of warfare, fighting a fight that I felt had different meanings behind it. Have you ever fought a fight that was not yours? I stepped between two brothers. They were blood brothers. I got hit in an effort to stop the fight before blood was shed between them. But whatever happened between those two brothers was relational and within the family. So even thou blood was shed, pain was inflicted and feelings were hurt, there was still reconciliation between the two. Why was that so? They still had faith and love for each other because they were blood. They knew that they came from the same seed, same father and mother. Jesus reminds us that He is the one who shed the blood that covers us and brings us into His family. We are the family that will reign with Him in eternity. If it had not been for the blood of Jesus, where would we be? He makes us blood brothers and sisters. So we must live a life of love, joy and peace in pure holiness.

There were other warfare moments. Once I was serving in Iraq or Afghanistan there were bullets are all around my head. The enemy would kill you without hesitation. It is important that every soldier knows that God loves them more than they could ever imagine no matter where they are. He loves you in battle and out. He loves you throughout the remainder of your life. He will shower you in love more than you will ever know. God wants you to know that your faith can still stand strong when you get out of the combat zone. He will preserve you for a set time and season. Your life is not over because you are a child of God and a servant of the Most High God. So today stand tall and be confident full of faith in Jesus Christ with the purpose predestined for your life.

Jesus is showing us a land that we can possess. He is pointing out things that we need to do to glorify Him. Has God shown you anything yet? Has He shown you that He will order your steps if you just step out on faith. The same Jesus will bless you just like He blessed Peter for stepping out of the boat to walk on water. You have got to believe just like Peter did for that moment in time. He knew it was Jesus! Can you feel Jesus in your life? If you step out and feel like you're sinking, Jesus will reach His hand out and pull you up so you will not drown. Blessed be His Righteous and Holy name.

FINDING JESUS FOR YOUR LIFE!

MATTHEW 7: 13 Enter by the narrow gate; for wide is the gate and broad is the way that leads to destruction, and there are many who go in by it. Because narrow is the gate and difficult is the way which leads to life, and there are few who find it.

My friend, please pay attention. Jesus is the way, truth and life (John 14:6). It is time for you to find Jesus for your own life. Finding Jesus is not harder than navigating in a big wide field or valley. God will allow each person to be on various terrain and give help for you to find your way out! In fact, your grid coordinates are Romans 10:9-10, 1 John 1:9 and John 1:6. Use those grid points to navigate your life into the right hands. Your Bible is the word of God. Follow it and you will find Jesus in your life and an abundance of blessings. You will find our Heavenly Father in the scriptures. You can also find Him in a local church service on any day. See a pastor and ask Him to help you receive Jesus as Lord in your life. The Lord wants you on the right path of life. Enter the narrow gate; it is the representation of Christ's Kingdom. If you miss the narrow gate, you could easily find you're inside the wide gate. The wide gate is that gate that drains the life out of you. It is really the same road demons are on waiting to suck the life out of you. Be a champion in God's Army today for your family's sake. Get Jesus in your life for your children to be saved and so they can pass the blessing on to their children.

Children, you should honor your parents if you ever want to make a mark in life. Go to church and accept Jesus inside your heart and get baptized. While you are walking in darkness, put on your night vision goggles so you can see. Christians need night vision goggles to find their way to the right gate in darkness. The path might be difficult, but you can find your way. Ask the Holy Spirit to hold your hand.

Go through God's gates, not hells gates! Get directions from the Holy Spirit. Get in the word of God! If you want Jesus in your life, follow simple directions. Direction #1 Receive Him as Lord and Savior. Repeat Romans 10:9.

One of the most critical skills to have in the military is the ability to maneuver around obstacles and overcome challenges on the battlefield. Therefore it is of the highest importance and priority to have Land Navigation skills to find your directions in a huge open battlefield or course. Before you are tested on land navigation, you have to get trained on what to do in order to know your direction on a map. A map has several gridlines, several north translations and features that you must know in order to get through and pass the test. If you want to be successful in finding your way home, you must be able to read a map. Then you must have the confidence to find the path home. If you enter the wrong gate, you could easily end up in the devil's court.

Night Land Navigation is much more difficult in the day time, especially when there are other tasks involved. It adds more stress because you have to more thought and the right execution to complete it at 100%. Routes are so extremely dark that you may not be able to see the hand of your leader not to mention your own hand. We like to think that you could see God's hand directing us. Our God has different ways to direct us while we are on the path.

Sometimes it is at the gate where you get directions to which location and path to take. The gate also represents the place we call heaven, a place of thanksgiving, a place of worship and deep adoration. The gate represents a spiritual place of entry. Psalms 100:4 states "enter into His gates with thanksgiving, and into His courts with praise." What a blessing to be able to do so every single day of your life. We should always enter the presence of God with thanksgiving because of what He has already done. Another scripture says that "the gates of Hades shall not prevail against it". Matthew 16. Satan, hell and all of its demons can never stop the church because Jesus already defeated him. Jesus is eternal and has all power in His hand. His glory is forever and ever.

As a believer of Jesus Christ, evil will be unable to stop you from accomplishing whatever purpose God has for you. The enemy may delay you, try to deny and intimidate you, but it is all a façade. You are a child of the most High God. You need to understand it clearly in your heart, mind and spirit. You have power in Jesus Christ.

Our God allows us to see something in this wide gate so we can get an understanding of reality. The wide gate is the gate that can lead you to hell. It is a real place. It is not for the believer to worry about, only those who do not believe in Jesus Christ will end up in that place. Tell all of your friends today that they need to accept Jesus as Lord and Savior. We denounce and rebuke every measure of Hell and every evil spirit that presents itself against the saints of God and the blessings of the Lord. We confess and profess the name of Jesus to rebuke and destroy all attacks of the enemy. Hell is a permanent place of residence to those who do not believe. We pray that they change their mindsets to believe in Jesus Christ as Lord and Redeemer.

The narrow gate is the gate that leads to heaven, eternal life. Anyone who puts forth the best effort can remain on this path of the narrow gate. They just need to have faith. The Bible says "trust the Lord with all thine heart and lean not to your own understanding, but acknowledge Him in all your ways and He will direct your path." Most people don't try to stay on the narrow road if they experience a road block. They experience pot holes and deep ruts that they find themselves in after taking wrong turns and traveling on the wrong paths. God wants you to get on the best highway so you can enter into the best gate.

The military is positioned throughout the world. Every soldier that is currently serving and those that have retired travel daily to get to military installations as well. Most travel to the military base because that is the place of duty. Some, on the other hand, travel for jobs and shopping centers. What is so important about the installation along with its high security is the fact that you have to have an identification card to enter the main gate and all military gates. They have the same level of security and restrictions for access. If your identification card is not stamped and approved and authorized by the proper agency, guards at the gate will not allow you inside. This main gate is the proper gate for military soldiers to enter to get equipped for battle and to plan engagement against the enemy. In this gate you stay on the right track to defeat all the arrows that the enemy throws at you. In this gate, you have the capability to put armor on and fight back. In this gate, you get prepared for war. . Here you have all the resources needed to be successful. When you function out of your atmosphere and environment, it may not be to your benefit. That is why it is important to remain on the right path and entering into the right gate. You do not enter into the enemy's gate unless you have been prepared to do battle. You do not enter the enemy's gate unless you are totally equipped to destroy the enemy and his cohorts.

We do not have time to let something little or imaginary impede our vision and purpose of Jesus Christ, our Lord. The wide gate is symbolic of the path leading to hell. Stop and take an assessment of where you are in life. What are you doing every day to progress in the Kingdom? Who are you serving every day? We all need to know that we serve our risen Savior. Do you even know and care about where you are destined to go after this life is over? I never hear people saying that they want to go to hell. It is because God designed us to want Him and to want to live with Him forever. Today, ask God to remove the scales from your eyes so that you can get back on the narrow path that leads to heaven.

The key to getting through the main gate of Jesus Christ is repentance, obedience, sacrifice, and believing by faith that He is the Son of God. He is the only true and wise God that delivered us from God's wrath. It is high time to tell friends and family about entering into the narrow gate. It is the gate where Jesus will bless you before you enter and while you are entering.

JESUS OPENED MY EYES!

JOHN 9:13-15 They brought him who formerly was blind to the Pharisees. Now it was a Sabbath when Jesus made the clay and opened his eyes. Then the Pharisees also asked him again how he had received his sight. He said to them, "He put clay on my eyes, and I washed, and I see."

The word, 'blind' means unable to see. It can come from a condition called glaucoma. Glaucoma is an eye condition that damages the optic nerve. Blindness also means lacking perception, awareness and discernment. You've heard the expression before, take off the blinders. This means that something is right in the front of you and you don't see it. You have even heard the phrase, 'you can see if you really want to'. Nobody is fooling God. Every person needs to remove the blinders in various areas of their lives. Get real about your life and service for God. The question is where do you have blinders? You will feel better and live better when the blinders are removed. You see when those spiritual blinders come off, the truth is revealed and nothing can stop you from walking in the blessing. The word is illuminated and the truth comes forward. When the blinders come off, you are now in a spiritual zone that God has placed you. Can you see the things you have been missing all of this time? All Christians have to walk and speak the word as we encourage and help other people.

Today is the day to take your blinders off! They can be removed whenever you are ready on this day. Jesus is waiting to enter your heart right now. That is exactly what happened to the Apostle Paul when he experienced Jesus during his wicked runs to murder. A conversion was waiting on him. So get ready! You will know that you are ready to run for Him in service as soon as you accept Jesus as Lord in your life. In fact, the only way you are truly ready is when you accept Jesus as Lord and Savor in your life. He will be the one to give you permanent vision. Your eyesight and your vision will be restored for the remainder of your life and nothing can change it. Barriers and all kinds of obstacles will be removed. Start trusting in the power of the Holy Spirit.

I know living with the natural body you can see things and they seem so clear. But when you operate in the spiritual realm, God is showing you things that defy the order of the natural realm. He is the God of both supernatural and even the natural because He made us. I, like so many other people, have difficulty explaining it all. There is just no way to tell it all. One thing for sure is that God is in charge of the supernatural things that occur in our lives. He is the God of miracles. Things that we cannot control nor understand He is there to show Himself strong. He defies natural order because He is the Creator of all things.

A blind man was brought to the Pharisees because they were disturbed at the fact that Jesus had healed a man who was blind all of his life. The Pharisees did not misunderstand the miracle Jesus had done. They were jealous and felt betrayed by the people because Jesus had gain so much fame from healing and delivering people. Jesus had proved Himself to be the son of God. All of the evidence needed was present. However, the Pharisees ignored it because of their interpretation of the law. They ignored it because of the reputation Jesus had gained by the people. Sometimes in life when you are doing the work of God and you do well at it, jealousy strikes the heart of people you know or may not know. All this jealousy and thinking that they were supposed to enforce the law over the miracle working power of Jesus had no substance and no way of glorifying God.

Jesus tells us in Mark 2:27-28, that the "Sabbath was made for man, and not man for the Sabbath. Therefore the Son of Man is Lord of the Sabbath." Do not worship the Sabbath day but worship on that day and other days. God is telling us not to allow religious beliefs to keep us from helping someone in need on the Sabbath or any day. The Lord has need of your service. If a brother falls in a pit on the Sabbath, be moved with a heart to help him get out of that pit. The only true and wise God is not about to allow someone to suffer because of the opinions, false ideas and traditions. He does not allow a day to go by that His healing touch is not involved. He is our healer and protector. If you go to the hospital on the Sabbath Day, you will find that the Holy Spirit is there healing people. If you go by the nursing home, where people are lonely and in need of companionship, the Holy Spirit is there. If you go by homes where people are not able to get out of bed, Jesus is visiting that person on the Sabbath day and any other day. He will heal on the Sabbath and any day that He needs to.

In **Mark 3: 1-5 And He entered the synagogue again, and a man was there who had a withered hand. So they watched Him closely, whether He would heal him on the Sabbath, so that they might accuse Him of blasphemy, saying He is God. And He said to the man who had the withered hand, "Step forward." Then He said to them, "Is it lawful on the Sabbath to do good or to do evil, to save life or to kill?" But they kept silent. And when He had looked around at them with anger, being grieved by the hardness of their hearts, He said to the**

man, "Stretch out your hand." And he stretched *it* out, and his hand was restored as whole as the other.

Jesus heals again. This time He entered the synagogue and a man was there who had a withered hand. Jesus was under watch at this time by the Pharisees to see what He would do. And it is just like Jesus not to abandon anyone. He will not let you go broken when you call on Him. Jesus asks the man to step forward with His withered hand. He told the man to stretch out his hand. And he stretched it out and it was healed even better than the other.

The Bible says that He never sleeps nor slumbers. He is always on watch, looking for someone who needs a miracle. You see it was on the Sabbath when Jesus opened the eyes of the blind man. He will open your eyes anytime you need Him to. He will remove the scales of darkness from those that have the Pharisee mentality. He will remove the spiritual scales that work to keep you in darkness. Millions of people today need a touch to see again. They are missing abundant blessings.

You heard the story of the mule stuck in the pit. The owner never thought for a moment to leave his mule so He stayed all night, digging a hole wider and trying to pull the mule free. He knew if he left that mule in the hole, he would just die. That mule had a special place in the owner's heart. You see when we fall into a ditch or a pit God has a special place for us in His heart. He is there no matter what the situation is.

YOU ARE GOD'S CHOSEN VESSEL

Acts 9:9-14 And he was three days without sight, and neither ate nor drank. Now there was a certain disciple at Damascus named Ananias; and to him the Lord said in a vision, "Ananias" And he said, "Here I am Lord." So the Lord said to him, Arise and go to the street called Straight, and inquire at the house of Judas for one called Saul of Tarsus, for behold, he is praying. And in a vision he has seen a man named Ananias coming in and putting his hand on him, so that he might

receive his sight. Then Ananias answered, Lord, I have heard from many about this man, how much harm he has done to Your saints in Jerusalem. And here he has authority from the chief priests to bind all who call on Your name.

God chose you to do something in His Kingdom. You will know it when you seek after it. Ananias spoke to God saying that this man Saul could never become a Christian because he was murdering Christians. In his mind, it was absolutely impossible for a conversion to happen with this man Saul. How could a murderer be changed so instantly and be proven in God's eye? Only God had such answer. The living God can do anything. He reminded Him that Saul was a chosen vessel. God's power worked on Saul inside and on the outside. He was transformed by Jesus Christ on the road to Damascus. I am convinced that one experience with Jesus can convert any man, woman and child. He has the only true transforming power.

Ananias was surprised that God would select someone who was once an enemy of our Lord and God's saints. Saul had been a man who killed habitually because of Christianity. He hunted Christians down like dirty dogs to the death. Thank God that He still used Ananias to bless Saul. This man, whom God selected, continued the remainder of his life in the powerful anointing. By God's grace and mercy, he wrote two thirds of the New Testament. He went on several missionary journeys to witness to unbelievers and believers alike. He later established churches along the way in his missions. God can change anybody for His glory. God can change the worst of the worst. His compassions fail not. His power and authority can never cease. His power is all eternal and everlasting. He is flawless, infinite, perfect, infallible and all mighty. His mercy endures forever.

There is always someone in life that God leads us to for the working of His ministry. When the Lord sends you to a person to receive you, let them receive you. However, always be aware that it is God who chose you before the foundations of the world. He already gave you sight before you came into the earth. Sooner or later more people will have gained their sight. God is able to use anybody whether spiritual or non-spiritual. I believe that you can never be limited by your past, mistakes, hurts, or handicap. Do not let anything hinder you because you are a child of the Most High God.

When I was a young child, my mother use to say put the record on for me baby. She was referring to the old 45s size records that they used in the 1950's and 1960s. She would want me to put on artist like Mr. B.B. King, the Temptations, Stevie Wonder, and Mr. Ray Charles, the old school. They all had amazing talent. But it was something unusual about Ray Charles and Mr. Stevie Wonder. They both were legally blind. I must admit that when I saw Jamie Fox playing the role of Ray Charles it brought back memories of this legendary artist who captured the minds and hearts of people through several generations. What set Mr. Charles apart from other artist is his amazing talent demonstrated under disabled conditions. Most people would have given up on life and hope. Certainly many people would have allowed their condition to overcome them.

Mr. Charles captured the heart of millions of people with his singing and piano playing talents even with a disability of blindness. He could even pat his feet at the organ and sing like no other. But I believe even today the majority of his fans never really saw him as blind because he never performed like he was blind. To some, blind means the inability to see from the lens of your eyes. Blind means unable to see the break of day. Blind means lacking the ability to see your way walking from point A to point B. Blindness is a condition that disables a person and set limitations. I never knew Ray Charles's spiritual condition whether he knew the Lord or not, but the attitude he portrayed would make one believe that He knew about the blessings of the Lord. He demonstrated that there are no limitations. Christians should have the ability to sing praises to the Lord with a zeal that is unlimited and unparalleled. Christians should sing with a heart of melody that will reflect the light of Christ and impact millions influencing them to surrender to the Lord.

THE GOD OF A SECOND CHANCE

Act 9 Saul! Saul! Why are you persecuting me?
Thank God that He allowed me to have a second chance at

life. When I was a young boy growing up, there were opportunities to do things too easily that could have caused harm and danger. It could have resulted in me losing my life. I am grateful that God heard my cry and He saw my frailties and weakness. It could have been for the worst. The enemy can't wait to steal the life out of any particular person and their family members.

There were times that I had bullets flying over my head in a neighborhood that had no plans to establish peace and stability. Some neighborhoods are just that rough. It was my choice to visit that place called the "Bottoms." It was my choice to visit "cross town" where violent gangs hang out and cause disruption and havoc on the lives of innocent people. God is waiting on gang members to turn their lives over as well. He has no respect of persons. When you think you are about get stabbed or engage in stabbing someone or even participate in a shooting of any kind, stop and think on the goodness of God in your life and your family. God is real and God does exist. Don't listen to anyone who says the opposite. God wants to give you a second chance regardless of what situation you are facing. Trust in the Lord with all your heart and lean not to your understanding. Acknowledge Him. He will direct your path. Acknowledge to Him that you need Him for this second chance. He will come to you.

There are second chances for everything that God allows for His glorious purpose? It does not change just because you come into the ministry and call yourself a minister or servant of the Most High God. Trouble still comes our way. No exemptions exist! So open your eyes and seek God for a second chance at life. Life is not over! Your life has a new start! Take this new lease on life and move in God's Kingdom purpose. Thank God for restoration. Thank God for renewal. Thank God for changing a destructive and evil mindset. The Apostle had all those conditions. When he met Jesus is when he allowed himself to die to sin and be born again. You must have a conversion. In John, it says, you must be born again.

What do you think the Apostle Paul said when he heard the voice of Jesus? He said who are you Lord? Although he did not have a relationship at that time, he still acknowledged Him as Lord. I believe Saul knew something divine and spectacular was about to happen to his life that would transform him forever. At that very moment, Saul had been given a second chance on life. Jesus could have taken him but He decided to use Him to win souls into the Kingdom under the influence of the Holy Spirit. He has been given a second chance to set the record straight. Jesus gave Him a second chance to follow Him under obedience. Jesus gave Him a lifetime of ministry to substitute the pain and suffering he had caused Christians. He was a murderer, a man filled with hate for Christians, But God intervened and no longer could he hate and murder Christians. Jesus had converted Saul on the spot. Jesus made Him over for the purpose of the Kingdom. He made Him to be a witness to the transforming power of Jesus Christ. He made Saul and changed his name to Paul and sent Him on multiple missionary journeys to express the love of God.

The Apostle Paul was positioned by Jesus Christ Himself to shake nations that God might be glorified. He blessed Him and ordained the Apostle Paul to be fearless and truly committed to preaching the gospel. The Gospel was to be preached so that all captives would be set free. God opens the door to a second chance for all that call on the name of Jesus. It's time to go to your prayer closet and start seeking Him for your second chance. God is waiting for you to make a move so He can bless you. Do not wait on man or you will be waiting too long and may miss the timing of God for your life. Listen to His voice when He says move. No matter what happened in your past, God can change it for His purpose and for your good. You can have a second chance to preach this gospel and help deliver the lost. You can have a second chance to be successful in the community and be a positive role model. You can have a second chance at your marriage. You can shake the devil off of your relationship. God can fix it and ordain it for you to live a good life, long and joyously with your loved one. You can have a second chance at serving the right God. Who is your God? Are you caught up in religion and do not understand that you have been blinded by Satan and his demons? Cast them out of your life right at this moment in the name of Jesus. Call the name of Jesus right now! Call the Lord and ask him to deliver you. You have a second chance at accepting Christ as Lord and Savior. Do not wait another day!

Read Romans 10:9-10 **That if you confess with your mouth the Lord Jesus and believe in your heart that God has raised Him from the dead, you will be saved. For with the heart one believes unto righteousness, and with the mouth confession is made unto salvation.**

Say this: Lord Jesus, I repent of my sin. Lord, come into my heart and save me. I believe that you are the Son of God and that you bled and died for my sin and rose from the dead. I thank you Lord for everlasting life.

Take advantage of your second chance and receive Jesus as Lord in your life. Tell 100 or more people about your conversion and how good God is. The Bible clearly shows us even with the rich man that second chances are something you just do not pass up with God. A second chance is a blessing that all friends and family can witness.

FAULTLESS

Jude 1:24-25 Now to Him who is able to keep you from stumbling, And to present you faultless Before the presence of His glory with exceeding joy, To God our Savior, Who alone is wise, Be glory and majesty, Dominion and power, Both now and forever. Amen.

God is able to keep us from falling into the enemy's hand. Every time the enemy attempts to make you stumble, speak the word: I can do all things through Christ Jesus who strengthens me. I am more than a conqueror through Jesus Christ, my Lord! All enemies get under my feet in the name of Jesus Christ, the Son of God. I present myself as a living sacrifice to God. All glory to the name of Jesus!

It is the Holy Spirit who presents us faultless before His presence. Think about it, we could never do what God can do. Have you ever found yourself where someone under the influence of the devil was trying to trip you up? In many cases, Christians and non-believers are tripped up on Sunday morning when the enemy keeps them from attending worship service at church. The enemy trips you up even when you find yourself purposely arriving late to church for a worship service. Everyone knows good and well that you have nothing to do on Sunday that has priority over God. You have absolutely no excuse for putting God second. Don't allow evil spirits to twist your mind and heart. So get up and go to the house of worship and praise His name. Blessings will flow in your life. Jesus has the power to keep you from stumbling and present you before His presence and His glory.

You could have fallen before and had no one to lift you off of the ground. Have you ever stumbled over your right or left foot and realized that you tripped yourself and quickly looked around to see who saw you? There are many occasions where people fall or stumble. Some people go out on military missions and they stumble when it's time to actually execute. Have you ever fallen accidently and it was so difficult to get back up on your feet? How about if you were in bed sick and just too ill to take care of yourself? I would seek after a Doctor. I would also keep my faith strong in the Lord. Some of us have fallen and people around us saw us and laughed. It always seems like a moment of embarrassment. Maybe you are better balanced than I am. The point is that in any of those circumstances, it is God the Father who picks us up over and over again. You never have to be embarrassed again. Our Father is gentle in heart and spirit. God wants us to depend on Him to sustain our lives and sanity. Have you ever fell to the bottom of life or hit the bottom as they say, because of an addiction? Have you ever fell spiritually from a relationship with Jesus Christ? Have you ever chosen anything or anyone above Jesus Christ? Ephesians 6:12-16 tells us that there are principalities and rulers of darkness. The Apostle Paul says, "For we do not wrestle against flesh and blood, but against principalities, against powers, against the rulers of the darkness of this age, against spiritual *hosts* of wickedness in the heavenly *places.* Therefore take up the whole armor of God, which you may be able to withstand in the evil day, and having done all, to stand." "Stand therefore, having girded your waist with truth, having put on the breastplate of righteousness, and having shod your feet with the preparation of the gospel of peace; above all, taking the shield of faith with which you will be able to quench all the fiery darts of the wicked one.

Many people have problems in their lives with drug habits and alcohol consumption which leads to so many improper actions and a wrong lifestyle.

APPENDIX: ROCK THE PEDESTAL

INTRODUCTION

Rock the Pedestal is about a man who finds himself in a situation where he has no option but to take a stand against crime and violence in the city. It has impacted innocent families including his family. Killers take innocent girls and women and sell them as sex slaves. These killers are involved in sex trafficking, murder, terrorism and cloning. Alex chases and fights on behalf of the city and country to bring down these villains that are in high places. He has a personal and special interest as well. A few years ago, his daughter was abducted and never found alive.

Greed is behind those things that keep people from having God truly in their hearts. Greed, power and corrupted positions exist in the city. Most of them are so corrupted and evil that they have no regard for innocent people and the poor. These crooks only place one another on a high pedestal in which they believe they are untouchable. Alex returns from war with his duffle bags and gets home to find out that his parents were killed during a police sting against drug lords and corrupted officials. He would later go to law school and become a lawyer.

This story opens with Alex trying a high profile case that involves high officials from the CID and FBI. There were efforts to lure Alex into this agency to use his skills. He rejected them; it was personal for the commissioner. Alex is against the government officials: CIA crooks, FBI crooks, and a corrupt police department along with hate groups associated with the law enforcement. The War Lord has his hand in everything.

Alex Rich is a man who just wants to party and make big money in the corporate business his parent left to him. He cannot let go of the tragic fatality of his mother, father and friends in combat. He also has bad memories of the assault and kidnapping of his sister. Alex suffers from Post-Traumatic Stress, as well. Nevertheless, he does not allow stigma and stereotyping attitudes interfere in his life. He manages quite well with these issues. He also keeps it under wraps due to his own pride. Alex never confesses it. He was a hero and does not want to appear weak. Alex is a strong man and honorable and believe in doing right by others. Alex wants to leave a legacy in the remembrance of his family and friends. A car accident was the cause of his parents' death. They were killed by a drunk driver as he was told. (In second paragraph, it says his parents were killed in a police sting). However, Alex does not believe it. He is now the inheritor of his father's estate and riches. He finds himself lonely one night. The next thing you know he's hanging out with friends in the club partying hard, dancing and drinking all night. His best friend, Danny met him on the football field the next morning, on the usual jog to the Mississippi track where they worked out. Danny had other persuasive friends that needed some special favors all the time. Alex finds himself in a situation deeper than he ever imagines after returning from Afghanistan and Iraq. His sister has been missing for weeks now and the case was put away and labeled as a cold case. Alex has constant flashbacks. Alex is faced with a rescue mission of women from a corrupted political system along with gang involvement and sex trafficking. The War Lord is behind this and his gang and people in every crooked place. Everywhere Alex goes, a hit man is sent by the War Lord in an effort to take him out.

ALEX'S APARTMENT TO TAKE SHOWER AFTER
RUNNING AROUND THE TRACK

Alex goes back home. He notices someone with a gun on his balcony. He saw him through the mirror. He plays it off. Alex walks casually in the other room as not to alert the burglar. But the burglar comes out and jumps him immediately, trying to kill him. They are entangled. The burglar has a firm grip around Alex's throat. But Alex manages to break loose and the burglar runs for his life. Alex did not realize with all the adrenaline flowing that he was stabbed in the side and bleeding heavily. The burglar runs out the lower level and breaks a window getting out. Meanwhile Alex reaches for his pistol in the secret compartment. He runs out to catch him; and shoots. The burglar got away too fast. Shots were fired and the police arrive at his home. A report was filed but Alex could not get a good look at the burglar because he had a tight mask on, even though the scuffle. Alex finds himself in a chase to catch these hit men of the war lord. Alex and the criminal driver go back and forth to avoid hitting other cars. A few cars flipped over and crashed. They exchanged gun fire from both cars at each other. A helicopter comes in to fire at Alex and protect the criminal.

ALEX'S OFFICE AT WORK-CORPORATE BUILDING
GUNMAN IN LOBBY SHOOTING

Alex is at work the next morning. As he walks in, he notices an unfamiliar face. He says to himself that he does not recognize the gentleman. Alice Mayes, the secretary is sitting at her desk. Then she greets Alex this morning, and brings coffee. "Alice, who is the gentleman that just left out of this section?" Alice replied, "What gentleman? No man has been here." "You have to be kidding me. He was just there. I did not see a ghost." The man is waiting outside to make an attempt to get the bag that Alex forgot to give

Danny. He is actually trying to kill Alex. Alex says, "Who are you looking for sir?" The strange man answers, "I am from the Daily Herald News. I am a news reporter looking for your CEO to do a story." Alex gives a look like, 'I know you're lying', but plays a long. "Well make an appointment at the front desk." Alex is leaving, the man walks behind him and takes out an automatic machine gun. Kelly White is screaming and people are ducking and diving to the floor. Some are running out of building, but being sawed down by this evil man. A gun fight occurs; the man is hit several times after firing at Alex. Three security guards were hit with rounds. After Alex shoots him, he searches his pockets. He found a mysterious code book and information about him. Detective Larry Watson shows up. "Sir", referring to Alex, "I am Detective Watson, I need to have a word with you. Can you tell me what happened?" Alex said, "It was simple, this man was following me and tried to kill me." Detective asked, "Do you know him or have you ever met him before?" Alex states, "No I have never seen him and do not know him." Detective Watson asked, "Do you know anyone who holds a grudge and is out to harm your family?" Alex says, "No."

ALEX'S IN THE PARK AND EYES ARE ON HIM

Alex goes to a park to investigate another body that has washed up. The police are all over the place trying to find evidence of what happened to this young beautiful blonde-haired woman. Just a few weeks ago, it was a beautiful black woman, a model of the Destiny Model agency downtown. Detective Brewster is on the scene and Alex shows up and asks some questions. Across the street, a suspicious character looks on and tries to walk away. Alex gets a glance and acts as though he was not going to bother him. However, Alex drives off and catches Sterling Gaines around the corner. He questions him about the murder and asks if he has seen anything. Alex says, "Where do you live and how often do you come this way?" Sterling says, "I just happened to come by this way and noticed all the cars. I have nothing to do with this." Alex asked, "Did you see anything at all suspicious?" Sterling says, "No. I told you, I was not here when this happened. Also, I do not like cops". Alex said, "I am not a cop. I will be your worst nightmare if you cop an attitude. I am looking for a killer. I can take you to the station." Sterling said, "Wait a minute. I did see a man with a long beard and dressed like he does martial arts." All of a sudden, a shot rings from a building across the street. Sterling is down. Alex takes cover and calls for back up and an ambulance. Alex proceeded to the building. The gunman runs and Alex meets this gunman at the top floor. The man falls from the roof as they scuffle. Alex tries to catch him. The ambulance shows up and the man is transported. Detective Brewster is at the hospital to question him if he comes back. A killer is in the hall way at University Hospital.

ALEX AT THE PRECINCT

Alex appears at the precinct to report to the CPT, Julius Martin, His boss. "Alex, I was just given a report that you pushed a man off a building. Everywhere you show up, there seems to be victims or bodies somewhere. I will take you off the case of these missing women since you are everywhere you have no business being." Alex defends himself and says, "I had to question a possible killer". Chief says, "One more incident with you and you're off the case. I will have your badge". "Thanks, Chief!" He leaves with some suspicion that Chief acts like he is connected to this.

ALEX'S AND TIFFANTY BACK AT HIS APARTMENTAND RESTAURANT

Tiffany knocks at the door of Alex's house. Alex answers the door and changes his entire expression because she looks so good.

She is halfway undressed to seduce him.

Tiffany says, "I just got back in town from Japan. I thought I would come by and see you. I told the cab driver to turn it around since I had you on my mind. I hope that is fine with you."

Alex says, "I am glad you turned around and made it here. Come in and relax. Can I get you a drink? Straight or with 7 up? She says, "Both".

Before they could even take a sip, love was all over the place. She embraced him like a serious cougar looking for a young man and steamy romance. It's on now. Kisses and sex all over the place. I hope no one gets hurt because there is a lot of noise in passion. Later these two would go to a restaurant. As they are dining in New York Eloquent Restaurant, shots ring out as they were enjoying their meal and conversation. They questioned whether they would be married one day or was this just a hot, steamy relationship.

Tiffany had mentioned before the shooting, that she didn't want any psychological games played in this arrangement. She said, "I am looking for more". All of this was said before the gun fire.

Alex was almost hit as the window shattered nearby where he was eating. A bullet barely missed both of them. They both got down. One shooter is inside and the other is outside. Alex crawls to the edge of one booth and manages to get a round off, knocking out the shooter inside, over by the women's room. He was disguised as a woman.

When the gun fire started, Alex's brain started to do something He started having psychological mood swings into a different man. He became a different person. He had a vision of that which was coming against him. Somehow he could see the opposing enemy in his mind with just one glimpse in the area. He had a gift intertwined with rapid impulses of Post-Traumatic Stress. The gift over rides all others.

Alex chased the second killer. He noticed a flashing red light directly on top of the building, across from the restaurant. Alex said, "Tiffany stay down, I will be back to get you". Alex runs to the nearby corner and shoots off a few rounds, then pursues to the other building. The shooter got away in a Corvette. He managed to get a glimpse of the tags. As Alex started to leave to get Tiffany, he was hit in the back of head, knocked out and thrown into a black van speeding at an alarming speed. They moved Alex to a warehouse where he is now being tortured for information concerning millions of dollars and top secret antidotes and codes that gives power to rule the world. Another hit man was in the restaurant. He receives a call to take her. One of the hit men grabbed Tiffany and put her in a separate van and took her to the warehouse.

ALEX'S IN WAREHOUSE-
KING PEN WAR LORD TORTURE ALEX RICH

War Lord Julius with his mask still on said, "So you are the one everybody has been talking about called Alex Rich. What are you rich in? I think nothing. Today you will die. Bring me the whip and board. I need some information out of you. Do I need to beat it out of you?"

Alex says, "Do what you need to do but you get nothing out of me". Julius said, "Are you sure?"

Julius says bring the girl to me. "Is this your girlfriend? I know she is". He begins to feel on her legs, and then kiss her in front of Alex. Julius says, "We will take extra care of her. I will personally take care of her after I take care of you Mr. Alex Rich. Take her back to the room. Tiffany is screaming and yelling as she is moved back upstairs and tied up. Alex told them to let her go. Some of the men are drooling over her. She is being taunted and sexually harassed.

After Julius has his hit men put a black mask on Alex and lay him down. They poured water down his face and mouth to drown him. At the same time, they were asking questions regarding the money, code and passwords. Alex did not give in.

Julius takes out his whip and has his hit mean to tie Alex to the running cables from the ceiling. "I will use this whip until you talk to me about the codes. I need to break into the system at the Central Intelligence Agency. You will give me the code or else I will beat it out of you and blow up federal buildings all over the world until I get what I want. I am the War Lord. No one wants to mess with me. You got that?"

One of War Lord's hit men has Alex tied up and standing by. Julius (War Lord) says "Move". He pulls back and strikes Alex with the whip on his back after pouring water on him. He hits him in the face several times (full fist) and Alex is bleeding. Alex takes the beating like a man and tells him, "I will kill you either way. I will search the world to kill you." The War Lord's men stretched the cable to pull his body and to break him. War Lord started another round of hitting him but Alex does not break. He makes only man sounds. Julius says, "Tell me the code and I will spare your life. Trust me, I will let you go free."

Meanwhile upstairs, Tiffany is being tossed around like a sex toy to three men each one eager to rape her. One man has already pulled her in the back room and pulled her clothes down, attempting to assault her sexually. Then his partner made him put back up the clothing.

Back downstairs, as Julius (war lord) pulls back to strike him the 5th time, Black Diamond, a friend broke down the doors of the warehouse with an eighteen wheeler tractor-trailer. At the same time Black Diamond fires a machine gun and grenade launcher. Black Diamond shoots with a 357 also. His buddy, Ray Killings (better known as Killer) previously created a distraction with a bulldozer outside to draw attention to the guards. Then he threw two grenades at the other end of the building, drawing them away to investigate. He takes his position and shoots from the other end. Both of them threw the enemy off and took out ten hit men. They had twelve enemy men down. Black goes in to free up Alex. Alex says, "Thanks man, but what took you so long?" Black Diamond says, "Can I get a thank you? That is what friends are for." Alex says, "Let's go!", as he rushes upstairs to take out the three other men. The War Lord Julius got away. He made a mysterious discovery that multiple women were being rushed and held inside of an underground cave. These bars were behind a secret compartment in which Alex somehow pushed the key section of the wall and it opened.

ALEX'S IN UNDERGROUND CAVE

Alex moves through the back entrance chasing War Lord. From a distance, he notices an opening that looks suspicious. Alex and Black Diamond discover a cave that leads underground. They cautiously went in. Alex says, "Black Diamond covers my back on this end". "Go, I have you covered". Alex keeps going. He hesitates at the three-way intersection of the underground tunnel. Alex takes the right turn. Black Diamond takes the left. Killer takes the center entrance. Alex keeps going and hears some groaning sounds. One woman hears footsteps and instinctively shouts, "Help!" To Alex's amazement he discovers women locked up behind bars in this cave. Most of them are tied up, half–dressed, and crying. Alex called Black Diamond, "Help me break every lock off these cages. Alex says out loud, "We are here to help. Don't worry". Alex says, "Ray call the police and FBI now! Give our location". Alex says, "Black Diamond take the left and I'll take the right. Blow all the locks off now! Go!" Alex shoots the locks off with a 357 magnum and 9 mm. He frees all the women. He brings them one by one to the holding points. The police and FBI arrive along with ambulances and medics. Alex knows that this is bigger than what he thought! "We need to get ready. We have a war on our hand. Greed and sex is involved. Someone is looking to make millions from these sex operations. The women have been tortured and need care and testing in the hospital. One of the women, Charlotte Campbell spoke up and said that she overheard the War Lord call out the word to Cuba to transport them and sell them to the highest bidder. He referred to Amsterdam and India, indicating that some would be shipped and sold there. The War Lord said that millions of dollars are in store. He already took at least 120 of the 375 women and girls here. Chief Daniels said to Alex, "Thanks. We will take it from here. Alex said, "Take care of them."

Alex had a history with Chief Daniels after returning from war, they had a fight in a bar, months ago. The FBI stated among the missing women, we do not have Barbara Canon in these groups. There are still some more women missing. The FBI, Mark

Bore said, "Thanks for your efforts, but make sure you do not interfere. We still have work to do. We will find this War Lord. He is a crooked FBI agent." He knew Chief Daniels had vested interest with the War Lord. Just months ago they seemed to make millions from a bank robber in Texas. Alex has a special gift to sense a person's heartbeat. If there are any psychological games, Alex can detect it with his gift. Psychological issues arise in the mind.

ALEX DISCOVERS THE EINSTEIN SCIENCE CENTER

Alex locates an underground laboratory of women being preserved through a process similar to freezing. The process was to preserve and clone for real world integration. This is done by a mad scientist name Dr. Bradly-Huntz Benton. The War Lord's head boss is trying to reinvent the minds of women and put them back in the population to test and see if society will notice the difference between the real women and cloned women. Dr. Benton wants to make women with new minds. The cloned women are to be made superior and will reproduce more babies and take over the world. "We can make over 2 billion dollars by creating this industry that has never been tapped into", says Dr. Benton. "I agree", says War Lord. "We will rule the world and be rich! You just take care of the project and I will take care of Detective Alex. It's my job to make this work. I have another partner for us by the name of Dr. Bill Fryer." Dr. Bill Fryer meets Dr. Benton. "This is my dream team. This will make the three of us rich. "Dr. .Benton, I am Bill and I have been working on this for the last 8 years. I will be delighted to work with you." "Thanks Bill". "Dr. Fryer, it's nice to meet you. I am Brad."

"Well we have a lot to talk about and plenty of work to do. He wants to control the world with his new invention, the model woman with the new intellectual mind. She can do anything and is stronger than the mutants." "I am not surprised at what he is doing. I need to catch him and put an end to this. We cannot have him trapping woman. Dr. Benton is in the process of creating a new mind that exceeds human intelligence in his view."

Alex says, "I know we can stop this project. Dr. Benton, how did you get mixed up with this?" as he is held up at gun point by Dr. Benton. "Alex, I knew you years ago. You asked me that question before. But what drives anyone? Money, sex and fame are usually rooted in corrupted people. I will have my name written in history books and the world will know me."

Alex asked, "At what cost? Do you really want to help the War Lord destroy societies and the world with clones?" Alex tells Detective Ronald Good over the phone that these people are evil and want to re-invent women with genius minds to repopulate and take over the planet.

Alex noticed through the walk around and investigation that there was evidence of a secret room. There was also evidence of women being tortured by forcing them to take cocaine, heroin and raped daily. Then he sells them on a ship that meets every 3 hours on the Florida coast. These women were being sold to countries such as Cuba, Spain, and the Republic of China. They were packaged up like commodities.

TWISTED- ALEX'S APARTMENT SEDUCTION

After a long day of being beat down, Alex goes back to his apartment, kick back and relax for a moment in the downstairs living room. To his surprise, the shower is on, champagne on the table with a dinner. Tiffany is in the shower. She is there to seduce Alex. Alex pulls his gun out and slowly moves toward the shower, wondering who is there. Knowing all along, it must be a woman. He knows Tiffany is held hostage. He notices a woman's body in the shower through the shower glass. Tiffany says, "Alex is that you?" "Yes." "Hand me a towel, please." She gets out and they hug with her towel wrapped around her. Alex says, "How did you get out? I thought they still had you." Tiffany says, "You should not underestimate me." They skipped the meal and wine and began heated passion in the bedroom. Alex is a little suspicious after she explained how she got away. Later at night, she gets up as Alex appears to be sleeping. She shoots at what she thinks is Alex. Alex is in another room. She moves to find him. Now she knows she is given away. She runs with her gun and silencer attached to find him in the house. Tiffany does her martial arts, fighting Alex. She hits him a few times and then he finally gets her in a position to keep her down. He gets out of the room. Alex's mother shoots off two rounds and takes Tiffany. (Mother was dead)   Alex is long gone but he recorded everything to his cell phone. Alex says, "Just what I thought. I got to admit the sex was good and thanks. I have to let her go. This is Alex calling the police department to let you know that Tiffany is not kidnapped and her location. Everything she was doing was to set me up for the kill. She was recording information and delivering it back to the War Lord. Tiffany is one of them." She was trying to seduce Alex to get the Code to the bank safe to give to her secret lover, War Lord. They were caught on camera together as well.

BAPTISM AND DEDICATION CEREMONIES
NEW HEAVEN'S MISSIONARY CHURCH

   Alex breaks away and shows up at his sister's home. He attended a baptism ceremony of his nieces and nephews. The Pastor preached his sermon on "A Man full of Faith in God". The Pastor spoke out of Genesis regarding Abraham. God used Abraham to exercise a level of faith and obedience. God simply wants us to possess the character that Abraham possessed. Simply put, when God asks you to trust Him, he wants your faith to be pure faith. Know that God hears you. Be the kind of person that will move when God speaks to you. Don't overreact to evil but you can react by calling on Jesus, the name above every name. He came from the same God that called Moses out of his comfort zone. It was the same God who called Jonah to preach the Gospel to a sinful city that he could have easily destroyed. He is the same God who told Abraham to leave his home, knowing all along that Abraham's obedience would help his family overcome struggles, and receive blessings in the land flowing with milk and honey. The Choir sings a song, "Nobody told me that road would easy. I've come too far from where I started from". Then they sing another selection, called "Stomp".

Pastor Zachery Conner calls, "Sharon, bring little Hope up here and dad come with them along with your family. Ralph and Bruce can sit here and they will be baptized immediately following the dedication. We will bless her in the name of Jesus Christ. Sharon your entire family can come". The Pastor places oil on the baby, symbolizing the blessings of God and the power of the anointing on the baby's life. "Lord, we ask you to bless this child under your mighty hand as you did for Hanna when presenting Samuel back to you. Bless this child likewise. Today this couple and the family pledge their faithfulness in the upbringing of this child, Hope, as a Christian in the church. She will learn the Word of God and the ways that God will direct her path. Parents, you are charged to take care and ensure she receives all the things in the church under the eyes of God. Likewise, Godfather and Godmother, your pledge is to also ensure her Christian development. Raise the child in the eyes of God, providing all her needs. The baptism takes place with Ralph and Bruce as the family looked on in the name of Jesus.

ALEX'S SISTER LEAVES CHURCH
CAR EXPLOSION AND GUN FIRE AROUND THE SECOND CAR

Alex gets into his car after the church celebration. He immediately recognized that his sister and her husband, Sharon and Michael Richards were safe and had no big worries. Both were injured in the car explosion, right before his eyes. Alex yells, "Move! Sharon!" Sharon and the baby were rushed to the hospital in an ambulance. Alex is inside the ambulance with his sister and the baby. He watches as paramedics work on her. Michael was closest to the bomb, but had no injuries. Both are rushed by ambulance. Alex is come down with Susan Reese, another close friend. The police and FBI are on site and are pressuring everyone because they want to get straight to the problem. They believe this single explosion and shells on the ground indicate a death threat, from someone wanting to get even. The burning explosion reveals that it was the work of a serial killer and his target is here.

ALEX'S AT HOME, LINDSEY KIDNAPPED AND DUMPED INTO ICE TO KILL HER

Alex is in a high intensity race to save Lindsey's life. He had to make decisions to put some things on the line. Lindsey is tossed through an open hole of freezing water which carries her under frozen ice. Alex only has seconds, if not a few minutes, before her body is frozen and she dies. Alex receives a phone call and note that warns him of Lindsey's danger, the person he loves. Alex says, "Do not touch my family? I will hunt you down and never give up until I kill you. Lindsay, are you home, honey?" Alex finds a note on the kitchen table that says here is your clue: Water fills the lungs and you can drown. Alex rushes behind the house. There is a pond that is frozen over behind his house. He shouts as he searches the ice for his wife. He runs to find an opening on the ice. Lindsey is kicking and knocking under the ice. He sees her body floating and eyes wide open under the ice. The ice is moving with her. She is hitting it trying to get out. Alex shouts again, "Lindsay, I am on my way!" He runs ahead several feet fast and shoots a hole. He runs back and tries to time her to get her out. Alex says, "Hold on, Lindsey. I am coming! He gets in with a rope tied to himself and tries to catch her. They both start sinking and losing oxygen. Black Diamond begins to pull them up, but start sinking again. She is still alive, but unconscious. Black Diamond starts up the truck and drives forward quickly pulling both Alex and his wife Lindsey to safety. Meanwhile the War Lord leaves a device to tell him that he would lose. A sniper is shooting at him as he rescues her. He shoots back as he tries getting her to safety. Black Diamond has his back on the other side, zeroing in on the sniper. Diamond nails the sniper. Black diamond pulls his wife to safety. Alex swears out loud to kill War Lord. "I will kill you!" Finally, Black Diamond shoots a volley of rounds and knocks out the sniper and War Lord's nest.

ALEX'S THE EQUALIZER INSIDE OF HIM
IN THE ENEMY'S CAMP- WAREHOUSE
OFFICE

Alex is so angry that he takes on the attitude of a vigilante in a sense. Everything he does at this point is similar to an equalizer who takes on all enemies. Alex is out for the reckoning. Alex catches up with War Lord and they both engage in confrontation. They go into hand to hand combat fighting with a form of martial arts called jujitsu. Alex gets the best of the War Lord. Eight of the War Lord men intervene to help him. Alex quickly beat each one of the War Lord's men and this frightened the War Lord. So he started to run. It dawned on him that this fight would never be over unless they finished it today. As the War Lord runs down the alley and to the open field, Alex is set up by an ambush on top of buildings in the alley and being fired upon. He uses his 9MM and keeps going. The War Lord is shooting at Alex as well. Alex is wounded in the shoulder but keeps chasing the War Lord down into a crafted maze designed by a science team of the War Lord. As soon as Alex enters the maze, the War Lord tricks him to engage with swords as he strikes at Alex upon entry and then runs at another part of the maze. The War Lord knows the maze, Alex is careful but the War Lord engages in fighting again with swords. They go back and forth. Alex rushes him and pins him with the sword. "You will not win", Alex says to the War Lord. "I am taking you out, now. You get to die, today because of hurting all of those women". They engaged again on the rooftop. The War Lord has Alex hanging halfway off the rooftop, clinging by one hand; War Lord was distracted by a few shots which caused him to run. Alex gets up with the help of Black Diamond. He chases the War Lord. They fight again. This time after mixing it up, at least three times, Alex takes the final strike and takes the War Lord out! Now he finds his way back out of the maze. Nevertheless, a surprise awaits him. War Lord has a twin. That twin gives Alex a new fight.

ALEX'S GOES TO A GRAVE SITE TO VISIT FRIENDS, COMBAT. AMBUSH AT THE GRAVE SITE: A CROOKED JUDGE AND COPS SENDS A HIT TEAM TO KILL ALEX

Alex is talking to old friends and combat buddies fallen in war at the grave site. "Well, my friends, I am back and hope you guys are in heaven. We had some wild times." (All of a sudden a helicopter with 8 men repel with weapons nearby) Alex runs back to the car to get fire weapons while under attack by these men. The helicopter pilot is also firing missiles to kill. He blew up Alex's car. Alex got out of the way in the nick of time. Alex moves to take cover behind a huge grave stone block. The helicopter hits it. It exploded. There was debris. Alex is slightly unconscious, but recovers fast. He gets up and moves toward a building for cover. Around the building is Ms. Sting, who is now shooting at Alex and manages to get a few punches in. Alex pushes her to the side and gets away. Black Diamond shows up with a Grenade Launcher. He shoots at the Helicopter and destroys it. He shoots at the corner of the building she is hiding behind and eliminates her. First shot, he missed. On his second shot, he takes the helicopter down. The enemy is upset. Now the CID and police fighters led by the top men including FBI agent, Daniel with a machine gun surround Alex and Black Diamond (combat buddy). They engage now with both Alex and Black Diamond, hand to hand. Alex fights with the attitude of an equalizer. He remembers it was War Lord and his men that killed Johnny Holms when they were illegally in the combat zone and mission. He remembers the gang ambush in combat by War Lords and his killers. They killed his buddies by setting them up and catching them off guard. The visions and memories continue to play in Alex's head when he saw that moment the CID and War Lord's men did harm to his friends and family. Multiple shots ring out. As people look around waiting, Alex was hit and was down on the ground. Alex shouts, "You will not put anyone else in the grave. Your turn now devil! After all the dust settles there were weapons everywhere. Alex is missing. No one can find him. They believe he was blown into pieces or burned up in the explosion. Alex was hit in the exchange of gun fire. He was injured, so he faked his death. Alex does not want this to leak. There is more corruption to clean up in the bureau. Alex and the FBI had a plan in place to locate this corruption and put to an end to it. So he faked his death.

ROCK THE PEDESTAL!
A NEW FIGHT- CHASING HEAD LEADERS

Alex rises up at the base of the river after the one corrupted member of congress had him tossed in a nearby pit for dead. Just when you thought it was over, Alex rises up and locates the underground tunnel where a secret office is located by War Lord's secret boss and a group of ISIS terrorist contact men. Not only are these terrorists lurking in the street, they have teamed up with War Lord and have ties to COL Chaney, a war veteran. These groups are not only terrorist with ties they are searching for gold and millions of dollars and will kill anyone that gets in the way! These things came about after Alex finds a document, from his search in one of the hidden offices. Alex goes back into the caves. He searches several locations to find that secret hidden compartment which contains more hidden women working as slaves for the crooked Senator, the Commissioner, and Alex's former Commander, COL Harry S. Chaney, one of his best friends in cahoots with His boss, Larry Sanders of the FBI agency, and last the head of the Mob, Rick Hayward. These are leaders who expect to be unstoppable. They are extremely corrupt and have plenty men to fight. No one has ever been able to touch these men sitting on a high pedestal. Alex discovers these men as he pushed this secret button underneath a large framed photo of COL Chaney inside the hidden caves. Behind it was another lever disguised as something else. Alex pulls this lever and new walls open and leads to a deeper compartment of the cave. The game has changed. Alex has to take this to a level of being a terminator because the big boys are deploying all arsenals. There is no return. Five of the guards of COL Chaney have spotted Alex and a chase is on inside the tunnels and caves. Alex reaches another section and takes quick cover for a moment. One guard sees him and the shooting begins with the sound of machine gun fire Alex returns a few shots and hits a fire extinguisher near one the exit, then he goes into hand to hand fighting again with seven men. Alex engages them with taekwondo, but he makes his way back up through the caves. He thinks he is clear. Alex has a bone to pick with COL Chaney. He looks back at the detailed, suicide mission security team that COL Chaney put him on. Three of his best buddies died instantly. Alex finally links up with Black Diamond for him. The Col and Alex fought behind closed doors in combat where he swore if we ever meet again it would be a show down. Alex hunts each one down…

ALEX CATCHES AND FIGHTS TERRORIST

Gunfire directed at a United States shopping mall. The president's family is shopping and eight men from a terrorist group hold up the shopping mall. They have other teams at the other end of the mall in four corners holding hostages. The President, the Governor, as well as the FBI are alerted that his family is in danger. The Secret Service has three men down. These terrorists are making demands that they have family members as hostages. They will start killing one by one if the money is not dropped off and if five prisoners are not released. Alex asks is this an ISIS group? Do you understand us? says the ISIS terrorist leader. The negotiators do not hesitate with killers. Alex moves right in. the FBI moves in afterwards. Alex goes in through the roof and surprises the entire terrorist group from each end. He gets on the handset and tells the leader of the gang that he was coming to take out the other crew. Terrorists holding at the west side of the shopping center try to anticipate Alex's entrance. Alex surprised each terrorist as they were in different perimeters. Then he approached the leader. Meanwhile the FBI is on the roof.

.

ALEX CAPTURED HIT MAN
BUSINESS OFFICE (SMALL SHACK)

Alex drives up a distance from the small business office and walks cautiously. Gun fire erupts toward Alex as he takes cover. After a few rounds fired off, Alex and the hit man go into a one on one fight. These two are both strong with talent to fight. He is the one who raped women and locked most of them in a dungeon. He also molested and killed innocent children. All Alex could think of was payback. He wanted to kill this murderer. Alex tells Rob to move behind the barrier in the hills and wait for a signal. I will take this fool out myself. One by one Alex beat each individual in hand to hand fighting. He is faster than the equalizer. One man had a karate style and engaged Alex. To his surprise Alex fought back with the same style. One minute later the fight was over. Alex struck him in the chest and damaged his heart and his larynx. Then he choked him. The fight was over and there was silence.

Later, Alex would be presented with a hero's award by the President of the United States and Governor, but he had to leave abruptly to save the life of another woman being tortured and threaten to be pushed off of a building. He was presented with the key to the city and the highest award the President can give for taking down Terrorists and criminals in sex trafficking. Alex is a hero and continues with new missions over the radio. Alex drives off with a new woman he loves.

www.ingramcontent.com/pod-product-compliance
Lightning Source LLC
Chambersburg PA
CBHW070824250626
47170CB00006B/2201